BILLY the KID
Is Not Crazy

BILLY the KID
Is Not Crazy

by S. F. Guerra

with illustrations by James Davies

two lions

two lions

Text copyright © 2013 by Stephanie Guerra
Illustrations copyright © 2013 by James Davies

Amazon Publishing
Attn: Amazon Children's Publishing
P.O. Box 400818
Las Vegas, NV 89140
www.amazon.com/amazonchildrenspublishing

Library of Congress Cataloging-in-Publication Data is available upon request.
ISBN-13: 9781477817322 (hardcover)
ISBN-10: 1477817328 (hardcover)
ISBN-13: 9781477867327 (eBook)
ISBN-10: 1477867325 (eBook)

Book design by Vera Soki
Editor: Marilyn Brigham

Printed in the United States of America (R)
First edition
10 9 8 7 6 5 4 3 2 1

To Anthony and Mariella, with all my love.
In memory of Dr. Lawrence Sipe, the best teacher I've ever known.

BILLY the KID
Is Not Crazy

Chapter 1

"I spent sixty-three percent of last month grounded," I say to my dad's back. He heaves a big sigh and keeps typing. I take another step into his office. "That's not even counting when I was asleep."

"Mmm-hmm," says Dad, still typing. The bald spot on the back of his head is getting bigger. I stare right at it and think: *let Billy off grounding, let Billy off grounding, let Billy off grounding.* I picture the thoughts melting into a fuzzy little line going straight into his brain. He doesn't turn around. I kick the door.

"Cut it out, Billy," Dad says without moving. "I know you don't like being grounded, but you need to deal with the consequences of your actions." Words like *consequences* make me want to scream and rip the leaking stuffing out of the back of his chair.

"But Dad!" I can hear my voice creeping up into that horrible little-kid whine that no ten-year-old should make. But I can't help it.

Dad finally turns around. His office chair creaks loudly as it swivels. He presses his hands to his eyes like maybe when he looks again, I won't be there anymore. But I am. "Billy, *why* were you grounded for sixty-three percent of last month?"

I'm quiet, and I know we're both thinking of all the stupid stuff I did.

"Can I have another chance?" I ask.

Dad shakes his head. "But I'll cut you a deal." (Dad's a lawyer; he's big on deals.) "If you stay out of trouble for the next week, you're off grounding, and I'll take you and Keenan to Wild Waves."

"*Really?*" I say. Keenan (that's my best friend) and I have been waiting forever to go to Wild Waves. We made a pact we'd go on the Kamikaze Slide for the first time together. It's this waterslide that goes straight down for like three hundred feet and dumps you in this huge pool. A kid broke both legs on it last summer.

"Yes, really. Just stay away from trouble; that's all you have to do." Dad gives me a hard look. "That means no cousin of trouble, not even an imaginary friend of trouble." Then he waves me away and turns back to his computer.

I get out of there fast, before he can change his mind. Wild Waves will be awesome . . . but I'm still stuck in this boredom machine for another week.

I head to the kitchen, where my mom and sisters are hanging out. Adrienne is thirteen and Betty's six, but they're the pukey-perfect twins who never get in trouble. They even look alike, with snobby noses and freckles, and they both love horses. But the thing they have most in common is that they think I'm an idiot. Right now they're helping my mom make soda bread. There's definitely a girl team in my house, but no guy team, because all my dad wants to do is read about Roman law and watch the History Channel.

Adrienne gives me a suspicious look when I peer over her shoulder.

"That looks like an arm," I say, poking her log of white dough. "A corpse's arm."

"Stop touching it," she snaps.

Betty has her own piece of dough, and she's sticking raisins on it in a smiley face. "It's the Loch Ness

Monster," she tells me. Betty is very into monsters, especially ones that people claim are still alive.

Mom smiles at me and keeps kneading her dough, humming something about a tractor. She's got her earbuds in so the rest of us don't have to hear her country music. Mom grew up in Georgia, where that's all they listen to.

I plop into a chair at the table behind them. Mom's phone is sitting there, so I take it off the charger, just to look for a second. I want a phone so bad. Adrienne got one when she was my age, but Mom and Dad say I'm still not ready, although they never tell me what "ready" means. I love the apps, but most of all I love the camera, because it can record video. Dad used to let me make movies on his phone, until I sort of erased a bunch of files. Now I'm not allowed to use it anymore.

But Mom never said I couldn't touch hers.

I switch it to camera mode and point it at myself.

Adrienne nudges Mom. "Billy's playing with your phone!"

Mom turns around, and I put it down really fast. She pulls out her earbuds. "Billy, that's not a toy."

"Sorry," I say. "I was just looking. Can I have a snack?" Saturday snacks are the best because they make up for some of the sugar and chemicals we miss on weekdays.

Mom nods, wipes off her hands, and dials the lock on the junk food cabinet. That clicking sound is better than the coolest song on the radio. It's better than an orchestra of angels. "Peanut butter or chocolate chip?" she says.

"Peanut butter."

She comes back to the table with a plate of the best cookies ever, which are shaped like peanuts and full of gooey vanilla stuff.

I take four. "Thanks."

"You're welcome." Mom gives me a close look. "You okay?" She can always tell when something's bugging me.

"I've been grounded forever. I think I might go crazy." Looking at Mom's face, I feel a little zing of hope. She feels sorry for me! There's no chance she'll override Dad, but she might let me do something else cool.

"You *have* been grounded for a long time," says Mom.

"I'm so bored," I say in my most pathetic voice.

"He's trying to make you feel sorry for him," Adrienne throws in.

Mom ignores her and pats my shoulder. "How about this? I'm not going to un-ground you, but once I finish the dough I'm going shopping at Wal-Mart, and if you want to bring Keenan, you boys can come along."

"Really?" I jump up and my chair goes flying. I stand it back up. "Can I call him now?"

Mom nods and smiles. "Glad you're feeling better."

I jet to the living room to get the house phone. While I'm dialing Keenan's number, I say a fast prayer that his dad won't answer. If Mr. Biggs could sell crazy, he'd be a millionaire by the end of the month. He's especially weird on the phone.

He answers. "Yeah?"

"Hi, Mr. Biggs, is Keenan there?"

"Who wants to know?" He's heard my voice a billion times, but he still asks the same question every time I call.

"This is Billy March."

"Hmm. Billy . . . No, don't know any Billy."

I sigh. Mr. Biggs is in a good mood. He's gonna mess

with me. If he were in a bad mood, he would have just hung up. "Billy, Keenan's friend."

"Billy, Keenan's friend," says Mr. Biggs. "That don't tell me nothin', boy. What do you look like?"

"I have red hair and green eyes, and I'm four-five, and I weigh seventy pounds, and I live at 980 Forty-Eighth Ave—"

Mr. Biggs busts out laughing. He must be in a *really* good mood. "Seventy pounds? You a little bag of bones, or what? Okay, okay, kid. I remember you. Hold on a second. *Keenan!*" He roars so loudly in my ear that I almost drop the receiver. "*Yo, Keenan!*"

Then another receiver picks up and Keenan says, "Hello?"

"Keenan, you got a skinny friend with red hair and green eyes who lives at . . . uh, wha'd you say, kid?"

"Hey, Billy," says Keenan.

Mr. Biggs chuckles and hangs up.

"Hey, man," I say. "You wanna come over and go to Wal-Mart with me?"

"Your mom let you off grounding?"

"Nah, not really. But she's going there, and we could probably mess around in the arcade while she's shopping."

"Okay." Keenan sounds a little bitter. He's never

grounded, but when I am, he's limited to boring stuff, too.

"Guess what else? My dad said if I'm good all next week, he'll take us to Wild Waves."

There's a silence. Then Keenan says, "A whole week? You gonna be able to do that?"

"Yeah!" I say. "For Wild Waves? Of course I am!"

"Okay, man." But Keenan doesn't sound like he believes me.

That's all right. I'll show him. "You coming over now?" I ask.

"Yeah, be right there." He hangs up.

I make a V with my arms for victory and jump in the air. Jailbreak!

Chapter 2

A few things about Keenan: he is very black—like black-black, not brown-black—and very short, and very smart. But he doesn't act like your typical nerd. You would never catch him raising his hand to answer a question, for example. And he doesn't like to admit he's in GATE. (That's a program for smart kids that we're in together. It's only once a week, so it's not too bad.) He's also the second-fastest runner in our class, even though his legs are probably half as long as most of the other kids'. But the best thing about Keenan is that he's laid-back. Nothing shakes him. Having such a crazy dad, he's already seen it all.

While I'm pulling on my shoes, Keenan knocks on the door. He lives only a few blocks away. I hop over and open it.

"Hey, Billy the Kid," Keenan says. That's a name I got last year, when we studied the Wild West in Mr. Ortega's class. The real Billy the Kid was an outlaw who did crazy stuff and got in lots of trouble. I guess I sort of reminded people of him.

"Hi, Keenan," Mom says from behind me. "That was fast. Give me a minute, and I'll get my purse."

"Yes, ma'am." Keenan calls all grown-ups *sir* and *ma'am*, which fools them into thinking he's good.

In a few minutes we're all packed into the SUV, which is the worst car ever. Adrienne calls it the Gas-beast and tells stories about dead baby birds and oil spills when she wants to get on Mom's nerves. Dad didn't want an SUV at all, but he finally said okay, if Mom had to be just like every other mom in West Seattle, we could get one. I said we should get a Lamborghini, but nobody listened.

"How's school, Keenan?" Mom asks.

"Fine, ma'am."

I fool with the electric headrest. Normally Keenan and I have plenty to talk about, but with Mom around it's like I got my tongue cut out and some evil good-kid zombie took over Keenan's body. Thank goodness Mom turns on the radio, even though it *is* country music. I stare out the window and try to tune out everything except the drums.

When we park at Wal-Mart, Keenan and I are both out of the car before Mom cuts the motor. Keenan chops his arms down and slices his leg into the air. "Who am I?"

"Fat Li!" I yell. That's our favorite character from *Ninja Warlords*, the best arcade game ever.

"You going to wish you wah nev-ah born," says Keenan in a terrible Japanese accent.

"Quit goofing before you get run over," says Mom. "Come on."

"What time should we meet you back here?" I ask. "We're going to the arcade."

Maybe it's the way I said it, kind of confident, that makes Mom feel like she has to take me down a notch. Maybe she used up her whole ration of nice earlier. She shakes her head. "You're still grounded. You boys can go to the arcade next week."

"But Mom!"

"Excuse me? You mean to tell me I let you bring a friend to the mall even though you're grounded, and this is the thanks I get?"

I don't know whether to point out that calling the Wal-Mart center a "mall" is like calling a raisin "candy" or to just implode. I open my mouth, and all that comes out is another "But!"

"No more *buts*, mister. Come on. Don't make me sorry I let you bring Keenan." That's an old parent trick: Bring the friend into it. Then the kid will shut up out of sheer embarrassment.

I look at Keenan, ready to bust.

He shrugs, which says it all: *calm down; no problem; it's cool.* Nothing fazes Keenan.

I shrug back at him, and we follow Mom into the store. She grabs a cart and starts off down the center aisle. We practically have to jog to keep up.

If I could pick anywhere to live, I would pick Wal-Mart. I'd live in the camping section, in one of the tents, and I would eat candy bars and potato chips every day for dinner and play video games on the big screen TVs. And I would watch movies—every single movie they have, especially the ones Mom and Dad say I'm too young for. If I got tired of sitting, I would go to the sporting goods section and play Wiffle ball and ride bikes through the store.

Mom must feel a little bad about not letting us go to the arcade, or else she wants to get rid of us, because she stops at the toy aisle and says, "You boys can stick around here if you want. I'll be back in half an hour."

"How come she's letting us stay here by ourselves but not the arcade?" Keenan asks as soon as she's gone.

I shrug. "I dunno. Maybe she's got it measured out by radius. Like if we're within three hundred feet of her it still counts as grounding."

Keenan pokes a Barbie in her plastic case. "This place is dumb. Everything's for girls and babies."

He's right. There are all kinds of dolls and baby toys and some cruddy plastic race cars, but not much else. Even the Slinky toys are in cardboard wrapping, so you can't play with them. I take a G.I. JOE off the shelf and point it at Keenan. "*Bpbpbpbpbpbpbp.*"

He takes one down and points it at me. "*Dtdtdtdtdt-dtdtdtdt.*"

We look at each other, kind of embarrassed. "This is lame," I say at the same time that Keenan says, "This is stupid."

"You wanna just hang out by the windows and play the car game?" he asks.

Keenan makes up cool games. He came up with this one when it was raining and we couldn't go outside. It's pretty simple, but fun. We sit and watch for cool cars, and as soon as one goes by, whoever screams, "Mine!"

first gets the car. There are other rules, of course, like if you scream "Mine!" at the same time, you have to have a wrestling match for the car; or if you accidentally say, "Mine!" when an *uncool* car goes by, the other person gets a free punch. The whole front of Wal-Mart has windows, and there's a section by the automatic door that's *all* windows. That's where we go, and we stand on a wooden bench right by the door so we can press our faces against the glass.

The game starts off awesome, because a Hummer and a Mazda RX-8 drive by one after another, but then we start seeing the same old Civics and Corollas. I zone out, watching the wind whipping trash all over the parking lot and people wheeling their groceries to their cars. People are funny: even if the cart stand is close, they'll shove their cart into some corner where it doesn't belong, like on the median or in another parking spot. It looks like this one scene in *Clone Wars* where all the labor droids are left on a field. . . .

What if the shopping carts really could think, like droids? That would be the worst, having to haul stuff back and forth every day, then getting left right where they could get run over by a car. They're at the bottom rung of their species, if you think about it. *Other* vehicles get motors, engines, horns, lights, leather interiors.

Shopping carts are just sad little grids of metal bent into boxes and put on small cruddy wheels for slave labor.

If I were a shopping cart, I would rebel.

"Mine!" shouts Keenan, but I don't even care that he bagged a brand-new Jeep; my eyes are on the empty cart slowly rolling down the parking lot.

"It's alive," I whisper.

"Huh?" says Keenan.

"The shopping cart! It's a droid, starting a rebellion! They're gonna wipe out the human race—we have to stop them!"

"Yeah!" Keenan says and jets out the automatic door. I never have to talk him into anything.

I admit it: there's a moment when the thought of Mom runs through my head. But there isn't really a choice. My best friend is out there battling an army of mutant (I realized they're mutant) droids, and I'm supposed to sit by and watch? If I were a commander in an army, would I wimp out when we met the bad guys? Heck no!

I tear out the door after Keenan.

I'm sprinting across the lot, cement slapping against my sneakers, cold air racing down my lungs. The droid is going faster, barreling toward us like a tank.

The car comes out of nowhere, and the cart smacks right into it—I mean *right* into it. There's a crazy squeal of brakes.

Suddenly nothing is funny anymore.

"Oh, crud," says Keenan.

My stomach clenches up, and my breath feels weird. The car door flies open, and this man jumps out. His face seriously looks like it's gonna explode; he is so fat and so mad. He's like the Michelin Man painted red and stung by a hive of hornets.

"You . . . little . . . turds!" he screams.

"Run!" yells Keenan, and he's gone. I mean, *gone.* But I'm such an idiot, I'm frozen, and when I do start to run, it's not fast enough.

The Michelin Man grabs my collar from behind. It's like a hangman's noose. *Chk.* I gasp for air, and my arms are flailing like they're still going somewhere.

"You're paying for my car door, you little turd," the man spits out. He leaves his car right there in the middle of the parking lot and hauls me toward the sidewalk.

And this is why Keenan is my best friend. *He comes back.* Dude is so fast he probably could have traveled back in time and gotten himself an alibi, but he comes back for me. He looks annoyed, like he got stuck with an idiot sidekick who needs rescuing, which I guess he did.

He looks at the Michelin Man and goes, "Come on, let him go. It was an accident."

The Michelin Man whips around, grabs him by the collar, and says, sort of snide, "Yeah, I noticed. Okay, buster, your parents can pay the other half of the bill. Or maybe I'll just let the cops handle it." The automatic doors hum open and he marches us into Wal-Mart.

I blink in the fluorescent light. The word *cops* pounds in my brain like a five-thousand-ton hammer. Did he say he was calling the *cops*? *Cops, cops, cops, cops* . . . My mouth is so dry it prickles. Somehow—I don't know how—my feet are still working, stumbling over the shiny floor.

Keenan yells, "Mrs. March! Yo, Mrs. March!" He's flipping around like a fish, but the man's still got the back of his shirt. I look in the direction he's staring. A lady in the same color shirt as my mom is turning down an aisle; it might be her, but it might not.

"Mrs. March!" Keenan bellows again.

"Who's Mrs. March?" the Michelin man snarls. "Is she supposed to be watching you?"

My eyes stay glued on the aisle where the lady disappeared. And then, like a movie in rewind, a leg comes out, and then a blue shirt, and then my mom's blonde hair. She sees the guy holding us, and she wheels around her cart and comes walking toward us, fast. "Billy," she says, and the look on her face is terrible because it's more sad than mad, and that's the worst look of all.

"What did he do?" Mom asks, not even looking at me. When she gets mad her Southern accent comes back, and it's really strong right now.

The guy is holding my arm so tight it feels like it might get pinched off, like an arm on a Play-Doh man. "This is your kid?" he says. "Lady, him and his friend . . ."

I tune out. I start counting tiles, looking anywhere but at Mom's face.

"I knew we wouldn't get to go to Wild Waves," whispers Keenan. I give him a dirty look. He shrugs, like *what?*

"All right, that'll work," says the man. "We don't have to involve the insurance company. I got a guy who can do it cheap." His voice is so nice he sounds like a whole different person. Mom has that effect on men, when she wants to. I look up, and sure enough, she's doing it: her whole face is looking all sweet and helpless and nice. I bet that Betty—my bratty little sister—will be just like that, and I'll have to spend my whole high school life fighting off jerks who want to go out with her.

Mom's face stops being nice the second she looks

at me, though. She pulls her keys out of her purse and holds them out to me between her thumb and pointer finger, like she's giving me a dead cockroach. "Get in the car," she hisses, "and stay there until I finish paying for the groceries. Do you think you can manage that? Do you think you can get to the car and sit inside for ten minutes without getting into trouble?"

I nod and take the keys.

The terrible thing about my mom is how *guilty* she can make you feel, like you put sticks in the wheels of a handicapped kid's wheelchair or called somebody's grandma a perverted cuss word. But she's right—I am bad. I'm never having kids, in case I end up with one like me.

The car ride home is the worst thing ever. Mom doesn't say a word, except for when Keenan says, "Sorry, Mrs. March," and she says, "I'm sure you are" in such a sarcastic way that even Keenan looks scared. Nobody makes a peep until she pulls up at his house and lets him out. She doesn't say anything about telling his dad, though. Mom wouldn't do that to him.

Keenan runs up the sidewalk, and then it's only a few minutes until we get home. All I can think about is *my* dad. He'll want to know why I did something so dumb, because he's a lawyer and he always wants to know my "motive"—except I never really have one.

He's going to give me his *look* and wait for me to explain. It'll be like we're in court. "Do you want to tell us exactly what happened when you wrecked the man's car?" he'll say.

Then I'll be like one of those guys he prosecutes, trying to get out of it, sweating, lying away.

"I was pushing the cart out of the way because it was about to run over a little kid."

"Sure you were. There were no little kids in that parking lot. What really happened?"

"I was trying to help take the cart back to Wal-Mart, but the wind blew it out of my hands and into the car."

He'll narrow his eyes. "The wind would have had to blow backward. Try again."

"Keenan hurt his leg and he couldn't walk so we had to ride the cart down the parking lot?"

"Keenan's leg healed pretty fast, hmm? I'm going to ask you one more time . . ."

"Billy, are you coming in?"

I didn't realize we were home. I jump out of the car.

Mom stands there, holding the front door open for me. "Why don't you take a seat in the living room? We'll sit down with your dad and have a nice talk."

Mom can be so sarcastic it's creepy. She disappears into Dad's study, and I go into the living room and sit on the farthest corner of the sofa. I know it's gonna be bad, but when I hear Dad say, *"What?"* all the way from his study, I start feeling sick. He comes stomping out with Mom right behind him.

"Sounds like you had some fun at Wal-Mart." Dad's glasses are pushed up on his head, which is a bad sign.

It is important to remember that anything I say right now will be wrong. I am playing freeze-tag, and I can't even blink.

The vein in Dad's forehead is showing. "Can you tell me exactly what you boys were doing?"

I shrug. My heart is going fast.

"Answer me, Billy!"

"Waiting for Mom."

"You were doing a lot more than waiting for your mother. I understand you pushed a cart directly into a man's car. *What were you doing?*"

Fine. He wants to know? I'll tell him. "Playing droid war."

"*Droid war?*"

"Yes, that's what I said!" Tears are coming. *No, don't cry.*

"I don't know what a droid war is, but do you realize that when you're 'playing,' you frequently end up destroying other people's property?" Dad is trying to talk normal, but his voice wobbles and he's obviously about to pop with rage.

"I didn't destroy anything! The guy knows somebody who can fix it cheap."

"Excuse me, but we're going to have a bill for hundreds of dollars. That sounds like you did some destroying!"

"I—"

"No!" Dad yells. "I don't want to hear anything out of you right now! I'm tired of your behavior! Your mom gives you a break from grounding, and *this* is what you do?"

I look at the floor. I am a big fat zero. My eyes are stinging, and I can't help it anymore, stupid tears are coming out, and it's not like I'm sad—I'm not. I'm *mad*, and I feel like I could just explode with it. I hate feeling like this, I *hate* it.

"Doug, calm down," whispers my mom. She's always trying to get him to be nicer to me, but she can't hide the truth. He hates me.

"I am calm!" Dad wipes his forehead. "Billy, apparently you haven't been grounded long enough. Let's make it longer. And forget about Wild Waves."

I can't handle it anymore. I run out of there and up to my room, and I slam the door as hard as I can. I wish I were bigger so I could slam it harder, so I could move out of here and never see them again, so I could break things and yell and kick and punch and nobody could stop me.

I'm *always* in trouble.

Chapter 3

There are some mornings when getting up feels like going to jail. For the last eight hours I was warm, asleep, dreaming that I knew how to skateboard really good and I beat Keenan in a contest, and now I have to put my feet on the ice-cold floor, go to school, and then come home and be *grounded*? Waking up is a pretty big rip-off.

But I pull myself out of bed and get dressed, because the last thing I need is to get in even more trouble for being late to school.

Mom and Dad are in the kitchen eating. I try not to look at them as I take out the cereal and make a bowl. The kitchen is very quiet.

Finally Mom says, "Billy, we told your sisters they could eat in the living room today. Why don't you go and join them? You can watch some cartoons if you want."

Cartoons? Before school? If you were in jail and the guard all of a sudden cooked you a big plate of blueberry pancakes, you'd probably think they were poisoned, too. So I don't much feel like watching cartoons. "Can I sit in here with you guys?" I ask.

Dad shakes his head. "Scoot, Billy. We're talking."

I try to leave the door open so I can hear what they're saying from the living room, but Mom gets up and closes it behind me. Adrienne and Betty are watching some dumb girl show.

What are Mom and Dad talking about in there? Reform school? Juvie? Giving me up for adoption?

Maybe they're going to take me to an orphanage and leave me on the step, like poor people used to do with their babies.

We ain't got any beds left, kid, so you'll have to sleep in the basement. You can be our Roach Boy. Everybody has to earn their keep.

Wh-what's a roach boy?

The kid who kills the roaches with his bare hands!

Roach Boy! Roach Boy!

I always hated redheaded kids, Roach Boy....

I *have* to know what they're saying in there.

Quiet as a thief, I get up and creep to the kitchen door. Adrienne and Betty don't even look up from their show. I stick my ear against the wood.

"It's a bad idea!" my dad is saying. "I don't want him labeled. And I don't think sending him to a—"

Mom interrupts. "You're biased. You know you are."

I feel like somebody punched me in the stomach. They *are* thinking about giving me away!

"I'm not biased. Remember Frank and Diana's therapist?"

Now I get it. They're talking about sending me to a shrink. Frank is my dad's brother, and last year Aunt Diana made him go to a shrink to talk about their marriage. Uncle Frank said it was the worst torture he ever went through and that shrinks are swami healers who figured out how to bilk the insurance system. That was at Christmas dinner.

Mom's voice gets softer. "Just because that one didn't work out doesn't mean they're all bad. I'm worried about how often Billy gets carried away by his imagination. A *droid war*? That is so strange. And there was that weird black hole game where he ruined the vacuum, and the robot game with Adrienne's computer, and . . . oh, I can't even keep track of everything over the past year. We need to at least get him evaluated. My friend Paula knows somebody good right downtown."

Oh, please no. Don't let Dad give in. Defend me, Dad!

"I just can't agree to this. They're not even real medical doctors."

"They go to the same amount of school. We need to do *something*. Remember what Mrs. Hawkins said at the last conference?"

"He gets perfect grades! What else does she want?" Dad snaps.

"For him not to distract all the other kids!"

Dad heaves a sigh. "I'll think about it. But can we give it a little time?"

There is a long silence. If I were a cartoon character, big bullets of sweat would be popping out all over me. *More time. Please say yes, please say yes, please say yes.*

"All right," says Mom.

I am so relieved I could melt into a puddle. The handle turns, and just in time, I take a few giant steps away from the door.

"Ready, guys?" Mom jingles the car keys.

I pull my backpack off the hook and cram in my homework and water bottle. Then I jet outside to get the backseat, because whoever sits in the front has to hold Mom's tea, and it always spills when she goes over bumps. She says it doesn't matter because it doesn't stain, but how would *she* feel if everyone she knows saw her looking like she peed her pants?

I'm shaky about the shrink thing, though, so I'm not in top form and get to the car last. Adrienne and Betty got their backpacks ready last night, so they probably would have beat me, anyway. That's how they are. They don't forget things, they don't break things, and then they rub it in.

"Hey, Flame Brain," says Adrienne from the backseat.

"Yeah, Flame Brain!" says Betty. They're always calling me stuff about my stupid red hair. Sometimes I wish they were boys so I could punch their lights out.

"That's enough, girls," says my mom, climbing in. "Red-haired men are the handsomest. That's why I married your dad." Mom is always telling whoppers to make me feel better, but I know the truth. Red hair is the worst, and so are freckles.

I get in the front seat because I have to and take Mom's tea. I want to tell her thanks a lot, I can't believe she wants to send me to a shrink, but I keep my mouth shut. I don't need to get in more trouble for spying.

As we drive, I stare out the window at the rain

smashing against the glass. Do my parents really think I'm crazy?

Everything is quiet for about two seconds, until Betty opens her big mouth. "Adrienne has a boyfriend," she announces.

"Do not." Adrienne is pretending to be annoyed, but you can tell she does have a boyfriend and she's really happy about it.

"Yeah?" says Mom. "No dating until you're sixteen, remember?"

Adrienne huffs. "It's not *dating* if I have a boyfriend. It's *dating* if we *hook up*."

Mom makes a funny sound, like a snort. "Hook up?"

Betty starts singing, "Adrienne and Ben, sittin' in a tree, K-I-S-S-I-N-G. First comes love, then—"

"So his name is Ben?" Mom asks.

"Why do you care?" says Adrienne.

"Well, because—wait a minute, why are we having a conversation about a boyfriend you're not even allowed to have yet?"

"Because you never said I couldn't have a boyfriend; you just said I couldn't date."

"Oh my God," says Mom. Mom never uses God's name in vain, so I know she's one step from losing it. Good thing we just got to school. She pulls over with a screech and Adrienne squeezes against the seat to let Betty climb over her. Adrienne is in middle school now, but Betty and I go to the same elementary school.

"Bye, Mommy," says Betty.

"Bye, sweetie." Mom reaches behind her seat to pat Betty's head and ends up whacking me in the face.

"Ow!" I say. "You're abusing me.'"

"Don't even joke about that!" Mom yells.

Cripes. I was just kidding.

I get out of the car, and my umbrella won't open. That's the kind of day it's going to be.

At least I get to my classroom before the bell rings. Mrs. Hawkins is the type of teacher who really cares if kids are on time. She has a chart with yellow stickers that she marks by the minute when you're late. So, if you walk in five minutes after the bell, she sticks five yellow stickers on your chart. When you get twenty in a week, that means after-school detention. That's not the only way she's weird, either. She has these X's of tape on the floor where the legs of our desks are supposed to go, and if your desk is off by even an inch, she puts a sticker on your chart. But on the good side, Mrs. Hawkins is fair. Like, she would never give somebody a good grade just because she likes them.

"Hey, Billy the Kid," Keenan says when I walk in.

I wish I really were Billy the Kid, so I could have adventures and not go to school. He was good at breaking out of jails, too, which would be a useful skill to have right now.

"Hi," I say. But I don't look at Keenan, because he can always tell when something's bugging me, and I'm not in the mood to explain about the shrink thing. I dump my books on the desk and start putting away my stuff: paper, pencils, and some white gummy erasers that I took out of Adrienne's room. She has art class in middle school, and she gets to use all kinds of cool supplies.

"What are those things?" somebody asks behind me. It's Mary Kazowski.

"Gummy erasers," I say, and I manage to sound sort of normal. Mary is the coolest girl in our class. At least I think she is. She doesn't talk much, which I like. She has long black hair, and her eyes are exactly the same bright blue as the water in my snow globe at home. "You want one?" I ask her.

"Really?" Mary picks one off the desk and mashes it between her fingers. "It's like Play-Doh."

"Yeah, except it erases stuff. Go on, you can have it."

"Thanks." Mary smiles. She's so shy she almost never smiles.

"You like her," Keenan says when Mary walks away.

"Do not!"

Keenan rolls his eyes. "Then why'd you give her your eraser? Don't even try, man. It's so obvious. You like her."

"Shut up! At least I don't like Rosaria!" Rosaria is this girl Keenan used to like who farted really loud in class a few weeks ago and stank up the whole classroom.

"Rosaria is prettier than your mom, dude," says Keenan.

Now why does he always have to bring my mom into it? That's his favorite way of ripping on me, to say something low about my mom. The thing is, he doesn't have a mom, at least not one he's ever met, so if I started ripping on her, he'd probably kill me. I think people should play fair in insult wars. Lucky for Keenan, the bell goes off and Mrs. Hawkins stands up.

First thing we do on Mondays is take a math quiz. Mrs. Hawkins claps her hands, and we sit down and grab our pencils. Math is easy for me—and boring. Right now we're converting fractions, which Dad already taught me two summers ago. It takes me about five minutes to do the problems on the board. Then I work on drawing a dodecahedron, which is hard because it has twelve faces. I'm trying to master all the polyhedrons, and I haven't got the hang of those yet. Finally Mrs. Hawkins collects the quizzes, and it's time for history. History can either be really cool or so boring it makes you want to rip paper into tiny pieces and throw them at the other kids in class. (That's something I got busted for last year. I was being a snow cloud.) When my dad teaches my sisters and me history, it's practically as good as watching a movie. He taught me and Betty about the Boston Tea Party by letting us dump a bunch of Mom's tea bags in the toilet until the water turned brown.

But Mrs. Hawkins is the opposite type of teacher. She makes us read out loud from a book, which is one of the worst kinds of torture there is—even worse than cafeteria-cleaning duty. Out of the whole fifth grade, there are probably like two kids who know how to read out loud. The rest of them never change their voice, or they read like one word an hour, or they mess up easy words like *although*. Sure enough, Mrs. Hawkins makes us all sit on the yellow rug (ugly, bright yellow, like somebody shot Big Bird and made a rug out of him) and open our books to the chapter on World War I. World War I is kind of the same as World War II: countries went crazy and tried to take over the world. Other than that, nobody really knows why it started, or how it ended, or what the heck it was about. Even the history book doesn't seem too clear on the subject.

"Dahlia? Would you like to begin?" says Mrs. Hawkins.

Criminy. Of course she picked Dahlia. Dahlia is the worst reader of them all. She never pauses for commas or periods, and she reads way too fast, to show how smart she is. Her voice is like some kind of giant drill that goes *whreeeee whreeeee whreeeee* into my brain.

"World War I began with the shot heard round the . . ."

I try to zone out and find something else to think about.

Shaquira Adams is sitting in front of me. Her hair is *interesting*. It keeps getting more complicated every week. The first week of school, it was a bunch of really tight braids. Then the next week, the braids got magically longer—like six *inches* longer. The week after that, the braids got piled on her head with some blue and yellow beads. Now they're swirled in patterns, like a hair sculpture.

". . . and because the Germans used the new tactics they discovered that . . ."

Dahlia's voice is like an ambulance siren; you can't *not* listen.

"They used code as a way to communicate some-times messages were hidden in menus at a famous restaurant in Berlin they would . . ."

Menus! Now that's cool. It just shows you can put a secret message in anything. I look down at my wrinkled old copy of *Land of the Free*. You could probably even put one in a textbook.

Hmm.

That would be the perfect place to hide a code, ac-tually. Secret agents with kids could be like, "Oh, son, I just want to see what you're reading in school," and nobody would ever suspect what they were doing.

I stare at the letters crowded onto the page in front of me. It's a warm day in Germany, and spies are sure to be out. I can't have them seeing me at work like this. I slump down and press my face into the pages. It's kind of nice, being hidden in this little cave of letters and musty, papery smell.

"Billy! Sit up!" squawks the fearsome German com-mander a few feet away.

"Sorry." I straighten up. My voice is cool; I look her in the eye.

Helga Von Hawkins (that's the name I retrieve from the face scanner in my watch) frowns at me, and then says to a young German girl sitting nearby, "You can keep reading, Dahlia."

Carefully, I lower my eyes. I stare at the words until they go squiggly and look like ants crawling around on the page. There are too many possibilities. Maybe every third letter is part of the real message, or every fourth, or even something more complicated, like only the capital letters. . . . What I need is a key.

I guess I could write one.

If I use exponents of two, and start with the first letter in the book . . . No, that's too complicated. It would be better to use pictures. . . .

"Billy March!"

My stomach goes *whoosh,* and I look up. Mrs. Hawkins is staring at me—I mean her evilest death stare. If I had any guts, I'd pretend to die right now from her laser beam eyes.

"What are you doing?" She stands. Her cheeks are red. She snatches my book. "Defacing school property?"

I guess I *was* writing in pen.

There isn't a single kid who's not staring at me right now.

"I dunno." My voice is a flea, a speck, a molecule.

"What do you mean, you don't know? I asked you a question. *What are you doing?*"

"Nothing," I tell her.

She looks down at the page I was drawing on and glares at me. "This is not *nothing!* What are these pictures supposed to mean?"

I shrug.

Mrs. Hawkins blows a hard *hmmsh* out of her nostrils. "Billy, I've had it up to *here.*"

Silence.

I want to ask, "Up to where?" but that would not be a good idea.

"Go sit in the time-out chair in the hall." Mrs. Hawkins's voice has a terrible sound in it, the one grown-ups get when they're right on the verge of losing it and screaming their guts out.

I head for the door. Keenan makes a pistol with his finger, the sign for *Billy the Kid,* but I don't look at him. People always think it's funny when I get in trouble, like I did it on purpose or something.

As I'm opening the door, Mrs. Hawkins says, "Your

parents are going to have to pay for this book. You can't erase pen. I'll call them after school."

I shut the door.

I'll call them after school I'll call them after school I'll call them after school.

How much are textbooks? Twenty bucks? Thirty? Fifty? Mom and Dad are going to kill me. Maybe this book was a really special one, and it'll be like a hundred bucks.

And then I think of something so much worse that I'd sign away all my birthday money until I'm fifty to make it not come true.

This will convince Mom and Dad to send me to a shrink. I just know it.

Chapter 4

I have never been this scared to walk inside my own house. Okay, that's not completely true; last year when I got busted for snorting Pixy Stix was pretty bad, too. I've been sitting on the grass next to my backpack for an hour, leaning against the big oak in our backyard.

This might be the last time I see daylight for a while. In some countries, if you steal you get your hand cut off. What if I lived in one of those countries? What would the punishment be for drawing all over a schoolbook?

Maybe they would tattoo whatever I wrote in the book all over my face. Maybe they would cut off my thumbs and make them into pens. Maybe they would

make me balance the book on my head and shoot it
off me. Maybe they would—

"Billy."

I whip around so fast I bonk my head on the tree.

"Are you okay?" Mom rushes over to check my head.

"I'm fine." I stand up, kind of shaky. Does she know?

"What are you doing out here?"

"I dunno, just sitting."

"Well, get up. You belong inside, mister." Her voice
is not joking.

Yep. She knows.

I grab my backpack and follow her into the house.

"You can sit down in the living room," says Mom.
"We have some talking to do."

It's kind of messed up, the way Mom and Dad
save the living room for all the bad talks. Living rooms
are supposed to be comfortable, not like torture cham-
bers.

I sit on the edge of the couch and play with the magnet toy on the coffee table.

Mom sits across from me. "Well, Mrs. Hawkins
called. Apparently we owe the school thirty-five dollars."

The way she's looking at me makes me wish I could
just crawl into a ball next to a garbage can, because
that's where I belong. "Sorry," I say.

Mom shakes her head. "Sorry isn't good enough. What is going *on* with you? Your dad and I are worried. Every time we turn around, you're destroying somebody's property. Last summer was a nightmare."

She's right. I am the stupidest kid ever born. I'll probably end up in jail when I grow up.

Mom sighs and rubs her eyes. "Why, Billy? *Why?* You know perfectly well that pen doesn't erase. And what were you drawing? Mrs. Hawkins said it was some sort of gagged football player! She's concerned! She wants me to pick up the textbook so I can see it myself."

A football player! I can't believe Mrs. Hawkins thought that.

If I don't explain, Mom'll really think I'm crazy. "It wasn't a football player, it was code. It meant *Red Hawk double-crossed us and captured agent twenty-eight.*"

Mom looks confused. "Red Hawk?"

I stare at the floor. "I was being a spy."

"A spy?" Mom repeats, like she can't believe I'm so dumb.

"At least I wasn't writing cuss words like some kids

do in the bathroom!" But right away I know I shouldn't have said that.

Mom's face goes dark. "This is not the moment to get fresh, mister."

She's quiet for a minute. I'm not going to say anything. Not one peep. Because whatever comes out of my mouth is wrong, and if I remember that I'll be a lot better off.

Finally Mom sighs and says in her sad, awful Georgia-accent voice, "Get in your room. I need to talk to your father about this. We'll be up to see you when he gets home."

I've been in my room for an hour and forty-two minutes now. No matter where I lie, my bed feels too hard, or too soft, or too lumpy. Mom brought me a bagel and lox earlier, but I can't eat anything even though I love lox. The whole room is starting to smell like fish.

Do Mom and Dad wish they didn't have me? Do they wish they could go back ten years and erase the night they *did it*? Do they wish I were a girl, because girls are easier than boys?

Or maybe they wish I were another boy. His name would be Stanley, because Dad wanted to name me Stanley, but Mom said he got to pick Adrienne's name so she should get to pick mine. Dad says he likes the name Billy just fine, but I've always wondered if that's really true.

Stanley would have blond hair and a tan and muscled legs that don't look like sticks. Stanley would have lots of friends, not just Keenan. He would never mess things up and break things, except once in a while, like on TV when the kid does something bad but it's funny and not really a big deal. I can *see* Stanley, in the kitchen, helping Mom get ready for dinner. . . .

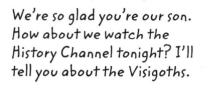

We're so glad you're our son. How about we watch the History Channel tonight? I'll tell you about the Visigoths.

It was sad when he died, but it was probably for the best.

We used to have another son, but he didn't turn out very well.

He was asking for it. He jumped off the roof wearing a cape. He was always pulling ridiculous stunts like that.

My eyes are stinging. I hate Stanley. If I really died and Mom and Dad had Stanley, I would haunt him. I would come to his bed every night and put my icy ghost hands all over his face. I think that's a lot scarier than saying "Boo." Boo is for Casper, not the Black Ghost of Night. That's who I'd be, the Black Ghost of—

There's a sound. I almost pee my pants, because for one tiny second I think it's the Black Ghost of Night. Then I realize it's a knock on the door—not a real knock that lets the person inside decide whether to answer, but an I'm-knocking-to-let-you-know-I'm-barging-in-whether-you-like-it-or-not knock.

Sure enough, my dad barges in with Mom right after him. Suddenly the room feels small.

Dad says, "Hey, guy" in this fake happy voice, and Mom smiles in a way that's more like she's stretching her lips than really smiling. Dad sits on my desk chair, and Mom sits on the bed, and I would pay every single penny I own, which is nine thousand two hundred eighty-three of them, plus whatever Mom and Dad have in my college account, to be somewhere else right now.

Dad leans forward and starts picking his nail. He's looking at me, but I can't stop staring at his hands because he just picked off a hangnail, and it looks like it really hurts. "Billy, we need to talk to you. We're not mad, okay? Let's get that clear. This isn't about punishing you."

I don't believe him for one second.

"We just want to ask you some questions," says Mom. "And we want you to be honest, okay?" Mom looks at Dad, and they both start talking at the same time.

"What did—"

"When you—"

Mom starts over. "Your dad picked up the textbook

on the way home. Can you tell us about those pictures you drew?"

"It was just code," I say, and my voice has a creak in it. "We were learning about spies in class."

They look at each other.

"When you drew them, did you really think you were a spy writing code?" Dad asks.

I shake my head. "I was just *playing*." I'm never telling them anything again.

"Well, it seems like when you're playing, you sometimes lose track of reality. Like when you said you were in that 'droid war' at Wal-Mart." Dad's voice is getting a tiny bit louder. "It seems like sometimes you get confused."

"I don't get confused! I'm not *stupid*!" I can feel my face heating up.

"We didn't say you were stupid," says Mom, putting a hand on Dad's arm. "I think we all know that's not the case."

That makes me feel a little better.

Mom says gently, "Can you just keep calm and talk to us? Can you try to explain what's going on in your head when you do this stuff?"

"Because frankly, we're worried," says Dad in a mad voice, but Mom shushes him.

I knew he was lying when he said he wasn't mad. His being mad makes every word I could think of saying crawl right back down my throat and hide in my stomach. I shake my head.

"No?" says Mom. "No, you can't explain what's going on in your head when you do this stuff?"

I shake my head again. I can feel my whole face freezing over, all the words icing down there in my stomach. I won't give them anything, not one thing. There is a silence that keeps stretching, getting longer and longer, but I don't care.

Finally Mom says, "Look, Billy. It's okay if you can't talk to us. But we need you to talk to someone. We're going to make an appointment for you to visit with a really nice guy, Dr. Greve. He's a child psychiatrist. He's somebody you can talk to about anything."

He did it. He sold me out. *Dad sold me out.*

"*I'm not crazy!* I'm not going to a shrink!" I scream. Mom puts her hand on my leg again, and I yell, "*Don't touch me!*" and I have the horrible thought that right now I *do* look crazy, because I'm screaming and losing it.

I clamp my mouth shut.

"Nobody said you were crazy," says Mom.

"We don't think that at all," says Dad. "A lot of perfectly normal people go to psychiatrists, just because they need someone to talk to."

That is the biggest lie I ever heard. "That's a lie," I tell Dad. "People go to *doctors* so they can get *better*. They don't pay a bunch of money just to talk to somebody."

Mom and Dad look at each other. They know I'm right. But Mom never gives up. "Look, it's true that sometimes psychiatrists help people get better, but they also help people avoid getting into problems in the first place. And sometimes they figure out if there *is* a problem at all. So if everything is okay with you, then Dr. Greve will tell us."

"It's just like going for a checkup with the regular doctor," Dad throws in.

He is so full of it. I want to tell him he's a liar, I heard what he said this morning, and I know what he really thinks.

"I'm not talking to him," I say.

"You're darn well gonna talk to him!" Dad snaps, and Mom says, "Doug!"

Dad takes a deep breath. "Sorry. We just need you to cooperate here, Billy. We're doing this because we love you and we're worried about you."

We're doing this because we love you. That's what they said last year when I had to start taking piano lessons. That's what they said when they wouldn't let me go to Horror Night at the movie theater.

Now I know for sure: I'm gonna hate Dr. Greve.

Chapter 5

Dr. Greve's office is *rich*. There's nice furniture in the waiting room, just like in a real house, and the seats are big, black, puffy leather. There's a red vase on the receptionist's desk with funny, bumpy things on one side. It looks like art—not good art, but the weird stuff in the modern art museum. Mom says modern art is for people who never learned how to draw, but Dad likes it. He says I'll understand when I get older.

I'm trying not to think about Dr. Greve. Have you ever noticed when you try not to think about something, it's all you can think about? Even while I'm trying to decide if the red vase looks more like an amoeba or a heart, Dr. Greve keeps sneaking into my head.

Greve sounds a little too much like *grave*, if you ask me. *Dr. Grave.*

"Billy March?"

It's a nurse—at least I think it is. She has a clipboard like a nurse, but she's dressed in normal clothes.

"That's us," says Mom.

"I'm Elaine. Come on back." Elaine smiles at us, and she's really pretty. This isn't at all like I imagined.

Mom touches my arm. "Do you want me to come with you, or would you rather talk to Dr. Greve alone?

He said it's whatever you're most comfortable with."

I don't want to go in there at *all*, with or without Mom. I stare at her with begging eyes. *Please don't make me do this.*

"Don't worry, Billy, Dr. Greve is very nice," Elaine says in such a sappy way that I know she thinks I'm a wimp. "Why don't you both come in?"

That's it. She *does* think I'm a wimp. "No, thanks. I'll go by myself." I get up to follow her.

Elaine holds open a door, and I march in. There's a terrible click as the door shuts behind me. I don't even notice the room I'm in; my eyes just zoom to the little man standing by the window. He looks like an Oompa-Loompa.

"Hi, Billy," he says in a voice that is way deeper than you would expect. His cheeks pudge up in a smile, and his eyes twinkle. *My shrink looks like one of Santa's elves.*

"Hi," I say.

"I'm Dr. Greve." He comes over and holds out his hand. He's trying to trick me into trusting him, but I'm not falling for it.

I shake his hand, but I don't smile.

"You want to have a seat?" He waves around the room, and suddenly I realize there are *lots* of seats, all different sizes, all different colors. There's a tiny rocking chair that only a kid smaller than Betty could fit into. There's a puffy blue couch that would be the perfect size for me and Keenan to play video games on. There are beanbags and a little lounge chair and even a papasan chair. I sit on the edge of the most uncomfortable-looking one: a wooden chair with no cushion.

I don't want him thinking he got me to relax.

Dr. Greve sits on the couch. Behind him is a giant—I mean *giant*—bookcase full of games and puzzles and books. There's even a set of paints wedged in there.

He crosses his legs. "So, Billy, what did your mom and dad tell you about why you're coming to see me today?"

I shrug and look at him. He looks right back at me. We look and look. I can't stand it anymore. I'm not good at being rude to grown-ups. I get this twitchy feeling in my stomach. "They think I'm always getting in trouble," I mutter.

"Do *you* think you're always getting in trouble?"

"I don't know."

"Well, let me explain a little about what we'll be doing in here. You're right; your mom and dad are concerned about some of the things that have happened lately. You and I are going to work together to figure out what's going on and come up with some strategies for staying out of trouble. Does that sound good?"

I narrow my eyes at him. It doesn't sound good at all. It sounds like all the grown-ups are a team, trying to figure out what's wrong with me.

Dr. Greve takes out a piece of paper and a box of colored pencils. "At the first session I like to spend time just getting to know each other. Sometimes I ask kids to play games or do some art. What I'd like now is for you to draw a picture for me, a picture of a person." He pulls out a folding table and sets it in front of me with the paper and pencils.

I look at the paper. There's a trick here, and I wish I knew what it was. He sure as heck doesn't want my picture for his refrigerator. *Draw a person.* He'll probably look at how big the mouth is, and how long the arms are, and what color I make the hair, and figure out all kinds of secret things about how my mind works.

I pick up a pencil and get busy. It only takes about a minute.

"Here you go." I lean back.

Dr. Greve picks up the picture and frowns. "This is a person?"

"Yeah, it's his shoe. The paper wasn't big enough to draw the rest of him."

Dr. Greve gives me a *look*, a one-eyebrow-up look

that I know pretty well. But all he says is, "Thank you, Billy. Why don't we play a game next? I'm going to start a sentence, and you finish it. You can say whatever jumps into your head, okay?"

Game, ha. He means *test*. I fold my arms. I'm ready.

"Once there was a boy . . ." Dr. Greve trails off.

"Whose name was Patrick O'Riley," I say, thinking of Betty's favorite story in this Irish fairy tales book our grandpa gave us.

Dr. Greve frowns. "This boy liked to . . ."

"Catch leprechauns."

Dr. Greve pauses for a minute and gives me a weird look. Then he says, "And when he caught a leprechaun, Patrick made a wish that . . ."

"That he could have his own farm!" This is almost fun.

Dr. Greve pauses again. "The other kids in Patrick's village thought he was . . ."

"There were no other kids in his village. He lived alone."

Dr. Greve sighs, a tiny sigh, but I hear it. "Thank you, Billy."

Then he leans back in his chair and looks out the window.

I look, too, and all I can see out there is another

building. What is he staring at? And how long are we going to sit here? I look at the little clock on the wall. Then back at Dr. Greve. Then back at the clock.

Dr. Greve isn't moving.

But then I catch him sneaking a glance at me, and suddenly I get it. He's waiting for *me* to say something.

Well, it won't work. I'm not saying a word if he doesn't make me. Not one single word.

A whole five minutes of silence goes by. Dr. Greve has one of the old-fashioned clocks where the hands have curly arrows on the ends. I stare at it the whole time.

Finally I win.

Dr. Greve says, "All right, Billy. I think that's a good start for today. I'll set up a time with your mom for you to come back next week."

"I have to come back?"

"Yes. Is that so terrible?" Dr. Greve gives me a nice smile. It's sort of hard to hate him, even though I want to.

He leans forward. "Look, buddy, I know it takes some getting used to, coming to see me. But you're not alone. I see twenty or thirty kids each week. Lots of people have times in their lives when they need a little help working things out. It's nothing to worry about."

"I'm not worried," I say.

"Good. Well, I'm looking forward to seeing you next time." Dr. Greve stands and walks me back out to Mom. I march past her, straight through the glass door leading outside. She almost has to jog through the parking lot to keep up with me. In case she didn't notice I'm mad, I slam the car door after I get in.

"Come on, it wasn't that bad, was it?" asks Mom, starting the engine.

"It was fine," I say in my meanest voice.

"Well, I thought he was very nice." Mom pulls out. "What did you think?"

I don't answer.

She darts me a worried look. Then she turns on the country station.

"I *hate* country," I say.

Mom sighs. "Stop with the attitude, Billy. I know this is hard, but that doesn't mean you're allowed to be rude." She turns the music down, but not off. "Why don't you tell me how it went with Dr. Greve?"

"I hate Dr. Greve."

"You *hate* him? Why?"

"I just hate him."

"You need to give me a better reason than that."

"All he does is talk about stupid leprechauns."

Mom looks confused. "Leprechauns?"

59

"Never mind." I cross my arms and stare out the window. I'm not telling her or my dad or Dr. Greve anything ever again.

It's me against them until I grow up and get out of here.

Keenan's dad goes to a shrink, so he knows a lot about them. I don't want to admit I already had to see Dr. Greve, but I need to find out what Keenan knows.

The next day at recess when we're sitting under the trees, waiting for a turn at tetherball, I say, as if it's not really important, "My parents said I'm so bad they might take me to a shrink."

"He'll give you drugs, man," says Keenan. "That's what shrinks do."

I pick up a stick and break it in half. "Like *pot*?"

Keenan doesn't even laugh, and that scares me. "No, like brain drugs. My dad takes them. It's like if your brain chemicals are wrong, the drugs will fix them."

A chill goes down my back. Maybe that's why Dr. Greve wanted me to draw a picture and play that weird game. He was figuring out what drugs to give me!

"There's nothing wrong with my brain chemicals!" I almost shout.

"Chill," says Keenan. "It's no big deal. You know Andrea? She takes them."

"But she's normal!"

"Yeah, because she takes drugs."

Andrea's the kind of kid you don't even notice, the kind who sits in the back and never talks and never gets in trouble and doesn't even look like anything special, just brown hair and kind of short. I really don't know anything about her.

"What kind of drugs?" I ask, trying to sound calm.

Keenan shrugs. "I dunno what they're called. She takes them so she can pay attention. I guess if she didn't take them, she'd go nuts and not be able to pay attention to the teacher or anything. That's what I heard."

"But I can pay attention," I say. "I get perfect grades."

"Maybe your problem is different."

"I don't *have* a problem!" I can feel my insides starting to boil. "There's nothing wrong with me! Do *you* think I have a problem?"

"Chill!" says Keenan. "You gotta chill out."

"Sorry," I say, because I really want him to answer me. "Well? Do you?"

Keenan grins. "I don't know. Maybe you do. Maybe you're *psycho*."

"*I'm not psycho,*" I spit out. And suddenly I want to punch him. Who does he think he is? Acting like he's so cool because he knows about brain drugs and I don't, and because nobody's telling him he's crazy. I get up and start jogging away.

Keenan jumps up and follows right behind me. "Wait up, man! What's your problem? I was just kidding! I bet you don't need them. Your parents probably won't even make you go; they're only trying to scare you or something."

"Whatever," I say. "I don't want to talk about it."

"Fine." Keenan stops right there in the middle of the blacktop and lets me keep going.

I don't know why I hang out with him, anyway.

I go to the water fountain and get a drink—a really long drink—and then I sneak behind the side of the building where we're not supposed to go because the recess monitor can't see us. I scrunch against the wall. The bricks are cold on my back. I put my head down in my arms because the wind is starting to freeze my face.

I'm a crazy person, and Dr. Greve is going to put me on a big metal bed and strap down my hands and my feet and turn on the shocker like in that one movie.

Suddenly I have to know. I'm burning, I have to know so bad. *What's the matter with me? Will Dr. Greve make me take drugs? What will the drugs do?*

I shoot off the ground, and I'm running around the side of the building, through the glass doors, and my feet are going *smack smack smack smack* on the tile, and I slam through the library doors right into Mrs. Olson's big, soft belly and there's an *oomph* as she lets out her breath and drops the book she was carrying onto the floor.

"Whoa! Billy, slow down!" Mrs. Olson says as I try to catch my breath and stop my body from moving. "Are you okay?"

"Yeah," I say. "I need some books. Can you help me find some books?"

Mrs. Olson laughs. "I wish every kid got this excited about reading. Sure, I can help you. What are you looking for?"

"I need a book about drugs."

Mrs. Olson puts her hands on her hips and frowns. "Oh, Billy."

"Not those kind of drugs, brain drugs," I explain. "Like the ones shrinks give you."

Mrs. Olson nods slowly. "Oh, you mean medication. I'm not sure we have any books like that. Is this for class?"

"I'm just doing research," I say, and it's not really a lie, because I *am* doing research.

Mrs. Olson smiles. Grown-ups love that word, *research*. "Well, I'll see what I can find for you, but have you thought about looking online?"

"Yeah," I say, even though I hadn't. "Can I use the computer here?"

The bell starts buzzing. Mrs. Olson looks up at the clock and shakes her head. "Billy, you better scoot to class. I'll keep an eye out for anything I can find, and I'll help you do an Internet search next time your class comes in."

"Can't we just look really fast? You could write a note for why I was late."

"I'm sorry, hon, but Mrs. Hawkins is going to worry if you don't get to class. Why don't you ask her if you can come back?"

I can tell she's not going to change her mind, so I jet out the door and back to Mrs. Hawkins's classroom. Everyone is walking through the door when I get there, and Mrs. Hawkins is standing in the hallway.

I go up to her, and the words want to come flying out of my mouth, but I stop them, because if I don't do this right, she won't let me go. "Excuse me, Mrs. Hawkins?" She's always telling us to say excuse me.

"Yes, Billy?"

"Can I go to the library? I thought of some research I need to do, and I want to get a book before any other classes go in there."

Mrs. Hawkins frowns. "What research? I didn't give you an assignment that requires research."

"Oh," I say. "Just . . . research." I think it might be the dumbest answer ever. But what am I supposed to say? *Actually, Mrs. Hawkins, my parents think I'm crazy and they made me go to a shrink and I'm trying to find out what kind of weird drugs he's gonna give me.*

"Billy, if you're trying to get out of class, that's a pretty transparent excuse," says Mrs. Hawkins. "Take a seat."

I go to my chair and sit down. Everything feels heavy all of a sudden, and I'm tired. Tired of people thinking I'm a liar, or screwed up, or psycho, or weird.

Maybe I am crazy. Maybe I am, and I just didn't know it.

Chapter 6

When Mom picks us up from school, she's in a bad mood because the haircut lady cut her bangs too short. I have to admit, she looks kind of silly, like one of those old-fashioned pictures of Grandpa with his hair in a bowl cut.

"It'll grow out fast," says Adrienne. "Probably just a couple of weeks."

"So it *does* look bad," says Mom.

"Not bad," says Adrienne. "Just weird."

"You look funny, Mommy," says Betty.

"*Funny,*" Mom spits out. "That's great; I look funny. I got this haircut for your dad's and my anniversary."

"Why do you care, anyway?" says Adrienne. "You guys are both old. You shouldn't worry about how you look. That's *vain*."

Mom frowns in the rearview. "What are you talking about, *old*? I'm forty-two."

"Forty-two is old, Mom," I tell her.

"I am *not* old!" says Mom, except it comes out more like "Ah am naht awld." Uh-oh. The Georgia accent. "I had a baby six years ago, okay? That's not old!"

"Then why do you have all those wrinkles?" asks Adrienne.

There is a big silence. Mom drives faster.

It must be terrible to get old, and kind of fat, and get gray in your hair, and wear dumb clothes. Old people never wear cool clothes. I will when I'm old, though. I'll have a job, so I'll have enough money to buy those red Nikes, the Speed Sharks that Keenan got for his birthday. And I'll wear sweatshirts from different colleges, and I'll never wear belts. If my hair gets gray, I'll shave it off. And if I get wrinkly, well . . . I don't know what you can do about that. Mom is always buying creams and things for her face, but obviously they don't work.

We pull into the garage, and I jump out and race inside before everybody else. Usually when I get home,

I go straight to my room to drop off my backpack, but today I throw it in the laundry room and go to Dad's office. We're not allowed in there by ourselves *ever*.

Before I can think too hard about what I'm doing, I slip inside and pull the door shut behind me.

It's cool and quiet in here. Even the air feels different. I almost don't want to breathe. It's dark except for a few bars of light coming through the window shades. Dad's big law books are lined up on the bookcase, and his desk is shining. On the corner of his desk is his special bronze paperweight, a statue of a lady holding a scale—and the scale really moves when you put things on it. I reach out and brush it with my finger, and it tips way faster than I expected: *squeeee*.

I yank my hand back. Suddenly I'm scared. But I'm not leaving until I find out about the brain drugs.

I sit down at Dad's desk, sinking too low in his big leather chair. My shoulders only come a little past the desktop. There's not much on there: the paperweight, a picture of us at the hospital when Betty was born, and a mug full of pens. And Dad's computer. We're never, ever allowed to touch Dad's computer.

I pull it toward me.

It's a sweet Toshiba laptop, all shiny and new, not like

the scratched-up old Apple in the living room, where Mom is always looking over my shoulder to make sure I didn't accidentally-on-purpose start playing online games with guys in China.

I press the button on the side, and the top snaps open. The little rows of keys stare at me. I press the silver circle in the corner, and the screen turns green. Dad's password is already in there, hidden with asterisks. It takes me about five seconds to get online. I go to Google, and the cursor blinks at me like an eye, watching.

What do I type in for the search? My brain is starting to jam like it always does when I'm nervous. All kinds of thoughts race around too fast to catch. I don't even know the words for this stuff. Mrs. Olson said *medication* but that would get too many hits for things like Tylenol. I type in *brain drugs* and hit *search*.

I can't believe how many hits there are:

The Brain: Drugs Fool Your Brain

Timmons & Hamilton: Drugs, Brains & Behavior

BBC NEWS/ Health/ Tool to help find new brain drugs

Science Museum/Your brain/Drugs and your
brain

IAS Bulletin Article: The New Generation of
Brain Drugs and Anti...

Effects of Drugs on Brain and Behavior

Betterhumans > "Branching" Protein a Target
for New Brain Drugs

Brain – Drugs and your health

News for brain drugs

Crankydragon's Scratches: Brain drugs
fuuuuuuuun ;)

And those are only the first ten. There are 9,720,000.

My brain feels like it's already on drugs, it's spinning so fast. I only have a few minutes. There are too many here! How am I supposed to pick?

I click on the first one.

The screen zooms to a bright-colored website, all blue and red and yellow, with a guy looking at a brain and some funny Cheerios shapes that might be cells. There's a whole page of little black print. I have to lean close to read.

Drugs Fool Your Brain

Drugs change the way your brain perceives
pleasure by triggering a rush of feel-good
chemicals like dopamine and serotonin. Drugs
make you "high" for short periods, but they
leave your brain depleted of these important
chemicals—and make it harder for you to
enjoy real experiences. You can become
addicted, meaning you are dependent on a
drug to get through your daily life. Meanwhile,
the drug can have serious consequences on
your body and mind. . . .

"Billy?"

I don't think, I just slam the computer down.

"Billy!" Mom's voice is coming from the hall.

I don't know how I jump out of Dad's seat and get
over to the door as fast as I do, but suddenly I'm there,
and I have to slow myself down just to ease open the
door a crack and peek out. My whole stomach feels like
it's thumping along with my heart.

"Billy! Answer me *now!*" Mom is stomping up the
stairs toward my bedroom.

I slide out the door like a ghost, glide down the

hallway, and slowly turn the corner into the living room, where Adrienne's eating popcorn on the couch.

"Mom's looking for you," she says.

"Mom?" I call up the stairs. "Adrienne says you're looking for me."

There are fast footsteps, and Mom looks down from the balcony. "There you are. I was about to get upset. I thought you'd taken off from grounding."

"No, I'm down here."

Thank goodness Mom doesn't ask any questions. She just comes down the steps, patting her too-short bangs. "I need you to help me out. Can you polish some silverware for tonight? Grandpa's coming over. That can be your chore for the day."

Sometimes I think my parents had kids because they didn't want to pay for servants. But right now I'm so relieved I didn't get caught, I don't care. "Sure," I say.

"Great. I'll get the polish for you."

I stand and watch while Mom digs the can of polish from the cabinet, and pulls out the big wooden box of silver. The only time we use it is when Grandpa comes, because when he gave it to us, he said, "You better not let this rot in the attic."

Mom sets me up at the kitchen table with news-paper and a bunch of rags. "Just do enough for six table settings," she says. "And take a break if your hands get tired."

"Okay." My voice sounds small even to my own ears.

Mom looks at me. "You all right?"

I nod.

Betty pokes her face around the door. "Can I help Billy?"

Mom looks at the pink goop and shakes her head. "Not this time, honey."

"But I want to help!" Betty wails.

"You can clean my room with me later," I tell her, and she smiles. It's kind of cool having at least one person who actually wants to do whatever I'm doing, no matter what.

Mom winks at me. "Good idea, Billy." She takes Betty out of the kitchen and leaves me alone.

I open the can and dip a rag into the pink goop. The smell of chemicals fills the air. I pick up a knife and start rubbing, making magic like King Midas with the golden touch, except I have the silver touch. I'm only just now starting to feel better. Rubbing back and forth makes me calm down. But after a minute, I calm down enough to start thinking, and all kinds of questions run through my brain.

Was the website talking only about drugs like pot and crack, or about drugs that shrinks give you, too?

What's the difference between brain drugs and regular drugs, anyway?

What if people just *think* there's a difference but there really isn't one?

What if Dr. Greve makes me take drugs, and I can't feel good on my own anymore?

What if I get addicted?

I look down, and the knife in my hand is so bright it's reflecting pieces of sun onto the wall. I put it down and pick up a fork. Why the heck would anybody get addicted to drugs, when they could have peanut butter cookies or something? I bet drugs don't even taste good.

I might be able to get addicted to peanut butter cookies, though. Every day, one peanut butter cookie an hour, or I drop down and start twitching.

I rub the fork harder and try to *feel* how bad I need peanut butter cookies. They're the only things that make me happy. They dance around in my brain, and if I smell them, I start drooling and beating people up to get to them.

We got another junkie, Sam.

You're going downtown, kid.

Can I have another peanut butter cookie?

You ain't gonna see another peanut butter cookie for years. They don't make them where you're going.

"How's the silver coming?" Mom peeks through the door.

"Can I have a peanut butter cookie?" I ask her.

"No. You'll ruin your dinner. Speed up in here, kiddo. They don't have to be perfect."

I put down the fork and pick up another one. I still don't know what it's like to be addicted. I mean, I really want a peanut butter cookie after thinking so much about them, but I don't *need* one. I'm glad; I don't want to need anything.

If Dr. Greve gives me drugs, I'll show Mom and Dad the pill on my tongue every morning, and then I'll go *glug* like I'm swallowing, but I'll really hide it in my cheek and spit it out in the toilet later.

But I'll have to make sure that Mom and Dad don't realize I'm not taking my pill. I'll have to wait a little bit after pretending to take it, and then start acting like a robot kid. I'll make my eyes stare straight ahead, and say, "Yes, mother" and "Yes, father" in a weird metal voice, and I'll walk kind of stiff and never get in trouble.

Well, maybe only small trouble. Just so I don't really go crazy from being too good all the time.

The doorbell rings, and I forget about pills and drop the fork and run for the door. *Grandpa is here!* Betty gets to the door at the same time I do, but I shove her out of the way and pull it open.

"Grandpa!"

"Whoa, whoa, don't kill me." Grandpa holds the door to keep from falling, because Betty is wrapping herself around his legs.

"Hi, Dad," Mom says from behind me. "Betty, let your grandpa come in."

Betty unsticks herself, and Grandpa steps inside. He hands Mom a brown paper bag. "Lock it away, Grace. That's not for the kids, what's in there."

"What is it?" I ask. I can never tell for sure when Grandpa's messing with us.

"What do you want it to be?" asks Grandpa.

"Peanut butter cookies," I say, because they're still on my mind.

Grandpa shakes his head. "Sorry. They did a new study and found out that peanut butter cookies kill brain cells. I brought carrot sticks."

"No, you didn't, Grandpa," says Betty. "What's in there?"

"Well, it's not carrot sticks *or* peanut butter cookies, you greedy little monsters. You'll just have to wait and see." Grandpa gives Mom a kiss on the cheek and hangs his coat on the coat tree that's been missing two branches since I tried to climb it when I was seven.

"Hi, Miss Betty. Howdy, Captain," he says, touching his forehead. Somehow it's not stupid when Grandpa calls me *Captain*, even though I would beat up anybody else who tried it.

"Grandpa, read me a book," says Betty.

"Why don't *you* read *me* a book?" Grandpa says.

"I can't read!" Betty giggles.

"What do you mean, you can't read? What are they teaching you in school these days, how to pick your nose? I could read when I was *born*."

Betty giggles even harder. "No, you couldn't, Grandpa."

"Are you calling me a liar?" Grandpa swoops Betty up in his arms and carries her off into the living room. I can't believe how grown-ups always fall for it when little kids act dumb.

"Will you ask your dad to come here for a second?" Mom says to me. "Tell him I need help in the kitchen."

"Dad's home?"

"Yeah. He's in his office."

My stomach swoops. I hope I didn't accidentally move something in there. Or leave fingerprints on his computer. Big, greasy fingerprints just my size. I didn't eat chips or anything, did I? No. But what about the paperweight? I moved the scale, but did I move it back? I don't think I moved it back. I *definitely* didn't move it back.

I can't stop fidgeting as I knock on the door of Dad's office.

"Yes?"

"Mom wants you to help her in the kitchen."

I can hear Dad's chair creak and a second later the door opens. He's still in his suit from work. "Hey, kiddo," he says.

He doesn't know!

"Hey," I say.

"Tell your mom I'll be just a minute." Dad has this look on his face, this *weird* look, and all of a sudden alarm bells are going off in my head. He *does* know.

I go back into the kitchen and try to sound calm when I give Mom the message.

"Thanks, sweetie," she says. "Will you start rounding up people for dinner? Get Adrienne off the phone, and tell Grandpa to finish reading to Betty."

I go upstairs and pound on Adrienne's door.

Is Dad dusting for fingerprints right now? Looking for hairs?

If he finds a hair, I'm toast. My hair is like a stop-light. It's like a curly, red glow-in-the-dark sign that says *Billy was here.*

"*What?*" says Adrienne.

"Dinner," I say. "Grandpa's here."

"Just a minute." Adrienne sounds all annoyed. She's showing off. She must be on the phone with Ben.

I go downstairs, where Grandpa and Betty are lying on the carpet, reading the Irish fairy tales book for the eighteen-billionth time. "Dinner's ready," I tell Grandpa.

"The end," Grandpa says, and stands up.

"That's not the end!" wails Betty, but Grandpa is pulling her by the hand toward the dining room.

I follow them, and there's Mom and Dad, standing by the window, whispering.

They know.

"How sweet," says Grandpa. "Still whispering like teenagers."

"Oh, Dad." Mom actually turns red.

Usually I would be grossed out, but instead I'm happy. Maybe they *were* being mushy. Maybe they *don't* know.

"Where's Adelhaide?" asks Grandpa. He calls

Adrienne "Adelhaide" like he calls me "Captain," but I don't think she likes it anymore.

"I'm here. Hi, Grandpa." Adrienne steps into the room, and I watch Dad's eyes zoom in on her like two radars. He makes a big motion of wiping his sleeve across his mouth.

"*What?*" says Adrienne, like she doesn't know. She's wearing lipstick again.

"Don't play games, Adrienne," says Dad. "Wipe it off now."

Adrienne huffs and grabs one of the brand-new cloth napkins off the table and wipes it across her face. When she takes it away, her lips are normal colored again, but there's a big smear like melted bubblegum on the napkin.

"We'll discuss this later," Dad tells her.

"Why do you want to look like a clown, anyway?" says Grandpa. "Only clowns paint their mouths. And trollops."

"What's a trollop?" asks Betty.

Dad says, "It's like a scallop, but different. Now let's say prayer."

Prayer is great, because it's this one little second when we're all talking to God, not being mad at each other, nobody saying anything snotty. Everybody bows their head, and Grandpa says the blessing.

I add a quick prayer in my head: *Please don't let Dad find out I was in his office and please don't let Dr. Greve give me brain drugs and please don't let me get addicted to anything, ever.* Then, because it seems like kind of a selfish prayer, I tack on: *And please bless all the druggies. Amen.*

Chapter 7

You know when you're so full that your belly feels like it's a whole other person hanging around your middle? That's how I feel right now. It turned out Grandpa brought fudge in the paper bag, and after the first four pieces I probably should have listened to my stomach (*stop!*) instead of my mouth (*go!*).

I try stretching out in a different direction on the sofa, but no matter which way I lie, I feel like I'm going to pop. I wish Grandpa were still here so he could tell me a story. Actually, I wish I could watch TV. A good show, the kind Mom hates, with lots of shooting and car chases and bombs and stuff.

There's a chance, a tiny chance, that if I ask really nicely, Mom and Dad'll let me.

That's enough to get me off the couch.

Where are they, anyway? They should be done putting Betty to bed. I check the kitchen, but the lights are off. Upstairs in the bedroom? Sometimes they hang out in there and talk. And sometimes they do other things, too, which is the grossest, worst thing I could ever think of in the whole world, and there was this one really horrible time in fourth grade when—

Never mind. It's too nasty to even think about. But usually they just talk up there, so I go upstairs and knock on their door. No answer. Then where—?

There's a *shriek* from Adrienne's room and Dad says, "Stop it, Adrienne."

"No! You're such *jerks*! I hate you!"

I suck in my breath. I can't believe she called them that.

"You never believe me! Stupid Billy's the liar! He's the one who did it!"

Oh no.

"Billy is ten, Adrienne. You expect me to believe he's looking up information on narcotics?"

Did I leave the computer on?

"Yeah! My friend smoked weed when she was in

fifth grade. You think Billy is so innocent, but he's not. Kids know *everything* by the time they're in sixth grade."

"Which of your friends smokes weed, Adrienne?" says Mom, in a tight, freaked-out voice.

"That's not the point! I don't smoke weed! I could have a billion times, and I never did! But you guys don't even believe me!" Adrienne's voice cracks, and she starts crying, big gulps like she can't get enough air.

"I didn't say we don't believe you about doing drugs," says Dad. "But I *do* believe you were in my office, looking up information about drugs on the Internet. And that's fine, to look up information, but we need to talk to you about—"

"I have my own computer! Why would I use yours?"

"Because yours is full of filters."

"*Well, I didn't!*" There are snuffles. "Ask Billy. Just ask him."

"All right, we will," says Mom.

Suddenly I can't breathe; I can't move. The floor creaks, and I *can* move after all, so fast that I'm in my own room on the bed before they even get into the hall.

"Billy?"

"Yeah?" I call.

Mom opens my door and peeks in. "I need to ask you something." She comes in and sits on the edge of my desk, and I wonder if she can see my heart pounding through my shirt. "You weren't in your dad's office for anything earlier, were you?"

"Yeah, I told him to help you in the kitchen, like you said." I can't believe how calm I sound.

"But that's all? You didn't go in there and look up anything online?"

"No. Dad doesn't let us use his computer." I hear the words coming out of my mouth, and it's like it's not me saying them—it's some slick liar who could fool the cops, a lie detector test, anybody.

Mom nods and gets up. "That's what I thought. Thanks, honey." She pulls the door shut behind her.

Thank You, God. Thank You, thank You, thank You—

There is a horrible howl from Adrienne's room.

Am I really thanking God that I *lied*?

Then I hear footsteps running in the hall, and suddenly my door rips open like it's getting hit by a hurricane. Adrienne is standing there, her face all red and streaky and mean. "Tell them it was you!"

"What are you talking about?" I say.

"Tell them it was you who went on Dad's computer! I know it was you! It wasn't Betty, and it wasn't *me*!"

"I don't know what you're talking about," I say coldly. And for a second, *I believe myself.*

"You little liar!" screams Adrienne. "You lying brat!"

"That's enough, Adrienne!" yells Dad. "Get in your room." He pulls Adrienne out by the arm and shuts my door.

I feel cold all over. Whoa, I *believed* myself. I actually got mad at Adrienne for saying I did it. Is that what happens when you're a liar? You start to believe your own lies? If you can't trust yourself, who can you trust?

I start to get up. I'm going to tell Mom and Dad the truth. I have to.

But now I'm getting a choky feeling. I sit back down. I *can't* tell them. Dad is scary mad right now, and I'm already in enough trouble. Adrienne never gets in trouble. I'm sure she does bad stuff she never gets caught for. She deserves to get busted for something.

I don't even really like Adrienne that much.

But I *believed* myself. That's just creepy.

I get up and run out of the room before I can change my mind. Adrienne's door is shut and there's no sound coming out. I jet into Mom and Dad's room.

"I did it," I blurt out, and they both turn from where they're standing by the dresser and look at me with surprised faces.

"What?" says Mom.

"I went on Dad's computer to find out about brain drugs 'cause Keenan said Dr. Greve is gonna make me take them and I was worried I might get addicted and—" I can't talk anymore because my voice is breaking.

Mom comes across the room in a few big steps and wraps her arms around me. Then Dad comes over and hugs me *and* Mom, and I'm smushed between them. I'm so relieved I want to cry, but I suck it back in because I'm too old for that. Finally Mom lets me go, and Dad steps back. I feel a little dizzy but better.

"I'm very proud of you for telling us the truth," says Mom.

Mom and Dad look at each other, and Dad says, "I'll go talk to Adrienne." He leaves and Mom pulls me onto the bed.

"What did Keenan tell you?" asks Mom.

"He said shrinks give you brain drugs. He said there's a kid in our class who takes drugs because she can't pay attention. And Keenan's dad takes them, too."

Mom sighs. "It's true that psychiatrists *can* prescribe medication, but they don't always do it. Mostly their job is to talk to you, and help you work out things going on in your life. If they do prescribe something, it's medicine, not drugs."

"Keenan said it was drugs."

"No, it's—" But then Mom stops herself. "Well,

okay. I guess it is drugs. But it's not the same as bad drugs, like the illegal kind."

"But I don't want to take *any* drugs," I say.

Mom raises her eyebrows and kind of smiles. "Well, that's good. Just keep that attitude, kiddo."

Then the door opens, and Dad is back.

"Keenan told Billy about a girl in his class with ADHD," Mom tells him. "And Keenan's dad is on some kind of prescription, too. So the kids concluded that psychiatrists make people take drugs."

Dad sits down next to Mom. "Billy, I don't want you to worry about that. We're not going to put you on medication."

"Hold on, Doug," Mom says. "What about ADHD? What if . . . ?"

Dad frowns. "It can't be. He gets perfect grades."

"That doesn't mean anything. It's more about impulsive behavior, right?"

"What are you guys talking about?" I feel the madness boiling up all over again. "What's ADHD?"

Dad sighs. "It's called Attention Deficit Hyperactivity Disorder, and kids with it have a hard time concentrating. They get fidgety, or their imagination runs away with them, or they get hyper. . . . I think there are different kinds of ADHD."

"I can concentrate," I tell him. "I read five chapters of *White Fang* last night."

Dad smiles. "That's good, buddy."

"It is good, but we don't know if that means for sure you don't have ADHD. That's why we need to ask Dr. Greve what *he* thinks." Mom gives Dad this look, and Dad's face tells me he's still not completely on board with this shrink thing.

"If I have ADHD, will he make me take drugs?" I say.

Dad says, "We wouldn't consider it unless there was a *really* good reason."

I'm so relieved. Maybe Dad is still on my team.

"You have an appointment with Dr. Greve tomorrow, and we can talk about it with him. You can get the answer straight from the horse's mouth," Mom says.

"What if he lies?" I ask.

"He won't lie, honey, and neither will we."

"Okay," I mutter.

Dad pats me on the back. "Now, about the computer. You need to trust us enough to ask us what you want to know. And I promise we'll always be honest with you, okay?"

"Okay," I say. I want to ask, *How do I trust you not to get mad if I ask something you don't like?* But of course I don't. Because that might make him mad.

"Good. Now I think you owe somebody an apology." Dad looks toward Adrienne's room.

"Oh man, do I have to?"

He nods.

I drag myself out of the room. Adrienne won't be happy I told the truth. She'll just want to kill me. She'll probably come flying at me with her teeth and nails like a banshee from "Medieval Creatures III," and I'll have to run for my life.

I take a deep breath and knock on her door. I wait about half a second and turn around. *I tried.*

But before I can escape, the door opens, and Adrienne peers out. "What?"

"Sorry," I mumble, not looking at her.

Then Adrienne does something really weird. "It's okay," she says. "Thanks for telling Mom and Dad."

I'm so shocked I actually look her in the eyes. A nice-kid-zombie must have taken over her body. She nods at me. And for one second, I think maybe she isn't so bad after all.

Chapter 8

When I walk into Dr. Greve's office the next day, there's a McDonald's bag and a Super Big Gulp sitting on his desk. He wipes his mouth with a napkin, waves at me, and takes a long drink of soda.

"Soda isn't good for you," I say.

"I know, but it's delicious. What can I say?" He smiles.

That makes me like him a tiny bit. I sit on the couch, because that wooden chair hurt my butt last time.

"So how are you doing this week?" Dr. Greve leans back in his chair.

"Are you going to make me take drugs?"

He snaps right back up. "What?"

I look him straight in the eye. "Are you going to make me take drugs?"

Dr. Greve laughs. "I like how direct you are. Your mom mentioned you were concerned about that, but I didn't think it would come up so fast. No, based on what I know about your situation, it hadn't occurred to me to prescribe medication. Why do you ask?"

"I heard shr—psychiatrists make people take drugs." I keep staring at him. You can tell when people are lying by looking at their eyes.

"Only sometimes," Dr. Greve says thoughtfully. "Lots of times we just talk." His eyes are steady, not darting around or anything.

"What about if they have that disease where they can't pay attention?" I say.

"Do *you* think you have trouble paying attention?" he asks.

"No. I do good in school. I read five chapters of *White Fang* in a row. I play video games with my best friend from like four o'clock to midnight, every time I spend the night at his house."

Dr. Greve nods. "You do well on tests, too. I saw your academic records. And your parents and teachers say you can pay attention pretty well."

I shrug. "Yeah."

"Are there any times when you have a hard time paying attention?"

"No, I can *always* pay attention if I want to."

"Hmm." Dr. Greve frowns. "Are there times when you *don't* want to?"

"Well, yeah, if I'm bored. But every kid doesn't pay attention when they're bored."

"You're right. So what do you do when you stop paying attention?"

I pick at my chair cushion. "I don't know."

"Zone out? Think about other things? Make up stories in your head?"

I look at him like *come on.* "You don't have to pretend. I know my mom told you."

"I really don't know," says Dr. Greve. "Your mom said you make up stories in your head and then act them out and get in trouble. But how would she know for sure? She doesn't know exactly what you think. That's why I'm asking you."

He's right. Mom *doesn't* know exactly what I think. "Yeah, I make up stuff sometimes," I tell him.

"What kind of stuff?"

I shrug again. I know better than to answer that.

"*I* make up stuff sometimes," says Dr. Greve. "I make up stories for my kids about a cat ghost called Herman."

"You have kids?"

"Yep. My daughter is one year younger than you, and my son is three." He points to a picture on the wall of a brown-haired girl holding a little boy on her lap.

"Isn't three kind of young for ghost stories?"

Dr. Greve laughs. "I guess so. Mainly I tell my daughter." He runs his hand along the books in the bookshelf. "These were written by people who like to make things up." He points at a modern art picture on the wall. "That was painted by somebody who likes to make things up. What kind of music do you like?"

"Rap," I say.

"Well, rappers like to make things up." He smiles at me, and his eyes look twinkly and nice. "Making things up is good, Billy. The thing we need to work on is getting in trouble *when* you're making things up." He leans forward and puts his elbows on his knees. "So how are we going to do that?"

He's asking *me*? "You're the doctor!" I tell him. I wonder what Mom would say if she knew she was paying this money to Dr. Greve so I could do all the work.

"Yes, but you're the one who has to make the change. I want to hear what would work best for you."

"You could put a metal thing on my head that gives me electric shocks when I do dumb stuff."

Dr. Greve just looks at me.

"Maybe I could try to think about what's gonna happen before I do something," I say.

"That sounds reasonable. How would that work?"

I squirm in my chair. "I don't know. I could just try to think what'll happen if I keep imagining. And if it's bad, I'll stop."

Dr. Greve nods. "I like that idea. Why don't we try it? You can report back to me next time you come in."

"I have to come back *again*? When are you going to know for sure that I'm not crazy so I can stop coming?"

Dr. Greve laughs. "Billy, I already know you're not crazy!"

It's funny how those words make me feel as if my insides took off and started flying. "Really?"

"I don't think you're crazy at all. Not one little bit. But that doesn't mean our work is done." Dr. Greve smiles at me. "Now listen, I need to talk to your mom for a few minutes. We'll see each other next week, okay?"

"Can I stay while you talk to my mom?" I have to scrounge up all my guts to get out the question, but it's really important.

"Not this time, kiddo," says Dr. Greve. "Just give us five minutes, okay?"

"Okay," I say, but the flying feeling is gone.

Dr. Greve is going to do the same thing every other grown-up does: say stuff behind my back. Maybe he wasn't even telling the truth about me not being crazy. Dr. Greve holds open the office door. My mom is still out there in the same chair, reading a magazine. She stands when she sees us.

Dr. Greve waves at her. "Come on in, Mrs. March. Billy, there are some great books on that shelf over there."

I feel something rising up. *It's not fair.* I shove the thought back down and stand by the window.

He said I wasn't crazy, so why does he have to talk to Mom alone? Maybe they both know I won't take drugs without a fight, so they're figuring out a way to sneak them in my food.

I'll have to be on the lookout for little round things in my meat loaf, or hiding in my breakfast cereal. I'll have to open up every sandwich Mom makes me, and mush my hand around in the peanut butter and jelly to make sure there's no pill buried in there.

Or maybe she'll get really tricky and sneak it into packaged food. Like, maybe she'll slit open a granola bar package and sprinkle powder on the bar, and then glue the wrapper back on. I heard about these wackos who inject poison into candy right through the plastic on Halloween. Unless you see that little pinhole, you're dead meat.

The door to Dr. Greve's office swings open, and I hear him saying: ". . . was my pleasure. We'll see you next week."

"Thanks," says Mom. "Have a good weekend." She gives me a nod, and we walk through the glass door leading outside.

"How'd it go today?" she asks as we head through the parking lot.

"What did he say about me?" I demand.

Her eyebrows go up. "Excuse me, is that how you talk to me?"

I ask in a more polite voice, "Mom, what did Dr. Greve say in there?"

Mom opens the door. "Well, he doesn't think you have ADHD. He said you're highly intelligent, and most likely you're just using your imagination to entertain yourself when you get bored. He wants to try something called behavior therapy. So we're going to keep seeing him for a while."

I climb into the car. "He said I was highly intelligent?"

"Yes, but we already knew that. Don't go getting a big head about it."

"So I don't have to take drugs?" I say as soon as she's belted in.

Mom shakes her head. "No."

"What's behavior therapy?"

"He's going to help you learn how to think things out before you act. He's going to teach you decision-making strategies."

"It sounds weird."

"Well, give it a chance." Mom glances at me as she pulls out of the lot. "Okay?"

The madness is leaking out of me like a beach ball losing air. I feel bad for thinking Mom would slip drugs into my food. I remember Dad saying, *You need to trust us.*

I look out the window at the buildings downtown. "Yeah, okay." I guess I don't have anything to lose.

Chapter 9

"So my parents took me to a shrink, and he strapped me on this bed and stuck big metal things on my ears and turned on the electricity. It was crazy," I tell Keenan at lunch the next day. "I was like a person having epilepsy. And I smelled smoke, like a little piece of my brain was frying or something."

He is bug-eyed. "No way, man."

"Yeah, and it *hurt*. But I felt calmer after, you know? And I'm taking this brain drug that my mom has to shoot in my arm with a needle every night. It gives me crazy dreams."

"*Really?*" says Keenan.

I bust up laughing. "No. But you believed me, man."

"I did not! I knew you were lying the whole time!" Keenan kicks the leg of the cafeteria table. He *did* believe me.

"I was just messing with you," I tell him. "It wasn't that big a deal. We just talked."

Keenan eyes me suspiciously. "Huh."

We don't say anymore. That's another reason Keenan's my best friend: he knows when not to ask questions.

Except two seconds later, I can't resist throwing in, "The shrink said I was really smart. He said I could write books or be a rapper or an artist or something."

"Quit bragging, man," says Keenan.

I can feel my face turning red. I get busy taking out my lunch.

Keenan peers at my food. "Trade you for a tuna sandwich."

Every lunch, we go through the same thing. "You don't even know what I have," I say.

"I know it's better than tuna."

That's true. Keenan's dad makes the same tired sandwich every day. It's not even real tuna salad; it's just tuna straight from the can dumped between two pieces of soggy white bread. I get good stuff, like ham and cheese or PBJ, and Mom always throws in chips and a drink.

I rip off a corner of my PB and J and give it to Keenan.

"Thanks, man." He stuffs the whole thing in his mouth and holds out his tuna sandwich to me.

"Why do you always do that, even though you know I'm not gonna take it?"

Keenan shrugs. "Trying to be polite. Hey, if you don't want that, I'll eat the rest."

I hold my sandwich out of his reach. "Get off! I haven't even started yet!"

"Sor-*ry*." Keenan gets up and heads to the third-grade table, where this kid Jerry sits. Jerry lives on Keenan's block, and he wishes he was our friend so bad he would probably eat live cockroaches just to hang out with us. Every single day he gives the best part of his lunch to Keenan.

While I eat, I think about Dr. Greve. It was pretty funny that Keenan believed me about the electric shocks. I should have told him something even worse, like that they gave me brain surgery. Then I could have acted zoned out and not finished my sentences and drooled. *That* would have scared him.

Going back to class after recess is like doing the dishes after dinner: the bad thing wipes out the good thing completely. Mrs. Hawkins is strict about how we walk inside from recess, too; if anybody whispers one tiny thing we have to go back and do it all over again. Today we make it in after one redo, which is pretty good, considering Dahlia and her dumb friend Kyla have bigger mouths than parrots.

"Take out your science books," says Mrs. Hawkins when we get inside. "We're on page forty-six. When you finish reading the chapter, please do the review questions at the end."

Keenan makes a little barfing noise, but not loud enough for her to hear. He's right. For the next half hour we're going to die of boredom.

Our science book is called *The World Around Us*, and it's full of sappy pictures drawn by some guy who got F's in cartoon school. I mean, this is supposed to be science, right? We should see photographs of real stuff, like intestines and brains and guts. But instead we get these stupid drawings that probably don't even look like the real thing.

I open to chapter four, *Genetic Coding*. Mrs. Hawkins is doing her patrol down my aisle, so I stare into the book like it's the coolest comic I've ever seen in my life. There are little pictures of ladders coiled up like film, climbing to who knows where. Is that junk really inside me? Is it *its* fault that I have red hair? The book says: "Hair color, eye color, height, and many other traits are determined by genetic coding."

Money says *that's* in the review questions. I flip back to check. Yep, number one: *Please name three traits that are determined by genetic coding.* I can always spot the review questions. They're the stuff in bold, or in the boxes on the side, or in the first sentence of a paragraph.

I zoom through the rest.

Then I stare at the wall. I do a lot of wall-staring in school, waiting for everyone else to finish. I wonder how those scientists figured out what's inside DNA. Did they cut it up? I can't wait till eighth grade, when we get to dissect frogs.

I wish I could dissect something now. Maybe I have something in my desk. I reach in and feel around . . . pencils, erasers, crumpled papers . . . and then I find my stress ball, the one Mom gave me to use if I get antsy.

Dr. March is working on another top-secret government project, dissecting an alien egg found on Zone 12 in New Mexico. It's rubbery but firm, with strange squishy insides.

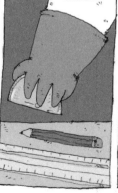

I'm guessing a plasmic life form, maybe carnivorous goo . . .

Thinking about being Dr. March makes me remember Dr. Greve. I pull the tip of my protractor out of the ball. I said I would stop and think about what would happen if I keep imagining:

A. Tons of tiny balls on the floor.

B. Black gooey stuff on the floor.

C. Weird gel on the floor.

Whatever's in there, Mrs. Hawkins does *not* want it on her floor. She gets twitchy if somebody drops a pencil and doesn't pick it up. I sigh and stick my stress ball back in the desk.

Then I watch Mary Kazowski for a while. She always bites her pencil when she's working really hard on something. Normally I would think it's gross, but somehow it's not when she does it. I wish she sat next to me.

But no, Donald Murray sits next to me. Dude fell out of the stupid tree and hit every branch on the way down. I feel sorry for him. He's always getting everything wrong, and you can tell he feels bad about it. Like right now, he's only on number two. Sure enough, he's writing *D*. I want to tell him the answer is *C*.

Should I?

I lean a little closer.

"Billy March!"

It's funny how your own name can sound like it's being shot out of a gun. I jerk back into my seat. "Yes, ma'am?"

Mrs. Hawkins glares at me. "Keep your eyes on your own paper. We do not cheat in this classroom. That's seven stickers."

"But I wasn't cheating!"

"Billy, I very clearly saw you looking at Donald's paper. Lying won't help the situation."

"But I wasn't cheating! I'm already done! Why would I cheat off *Donald*?"

There is a terrible silence. Then Oliver Mendez makes a pistol with his finger, whispers, "Billy the Kid!" and giggles. It's just a small giggle, but Donald's cheeks flame up even redder than they already were, and I wish I could turn into a desk molecule and morph into the desk.

"I *saw* you cheating," Mrs. Hawkins says, "and being cruel to your classmate won't change that. You may apologize to Donald. That's fifteen stickers."

Fifteen stickers!

"Sorry, Donald," I say in a low voice.

I feel like I just kicked a puppy. I shouldn't have said that about Donald. It slipped out. See? Stupid Dr. Greve was wrong. I even get in trouble when I'm *trying* to be good.

I'm such a loser.

But then I think: This mess-up doesn't count, because my parents don't know about it.

When I get home from school, Mom is on the couch with a stack of books from the library. The weird thing is, they're kids' books. I can tell by the covers. I sling off my backpack and head for the kitchen, but Mom says in this cheery voice, "Billy, would you like to come read with me?"

I stop and stare at her. Is she having some flashback to when I was in kindergarten? "I can read just fine by myself," I say.

"Of course you can, but it's still nice for us to read together." She smiles and pats the couch.

"No, that's okay." I start toward the kitchen again.

"Billy!" Now Mom doesn't sound so sweet anymore. "I'd like to spend a little time with you. I went to the library and got some great books. Is it too much to ask that you read with me for fifteen minutes?"

"I've already read those," I say, even though I can't see

what's in the pile. "Don't you have other stuff to do?"

"No. I really want to spend time with you." Mom smiles again, and my lie detector starts beeping like crazy. Suddenly, I know what this is about.

"Did Dr. Greve tell you to do this?"

"Billy—"

I roll my eyes. "Mom, I'm not a baby. I don't need you to read to me, okay? Tell Dr. Greve it was a dumb idea." And I march off to the kitchen, but not before I see the hurt look on her face.

I don't care. If Mom really wanted to hang out with me, she wouldn't need a shrink to tell her to do it. Besides, I wish I saw her *less*, not more. In fact, I wish she worked, like other kids' moms. Then I probably wouldn't get in trouble so much because she wouldn't be here to catch me.

I look in the refrigerator for a snack. Mom and Dad lock up the good stuff, but I've learned some tricks over the years. There are a few inches of milk left in the carton, so I dump in some Hershey's syrup and a bunch of sugar and shake it around till it's good and foamy. I'm just getting ready to chug it when I see Mom's phone charging on the counter. I unplug it and turn it to camera mode so I can film myself.

Do you want to show your kid how much you love him? Don't read to him.

GIVE HIM SUGAR!

I'm giggling as I put Mom's phone back in the charger. I don't think she uses the camera on her phone much, but maybe she'll see that one day and wonder what it is and watch it. I hope she'll think it's funny. I'd never try it with Dad's phone.

It's a good thing I figured out what Mom was up to, because Dad tries the exact same thing the next day, and I might have fallen for it if I wasn't ready.

It's Saturday, and he doesn't disappear into his office like usual after breakfast. Instead he breaks out an old football from the garage and asks if I want to do some passing.

This is an even worse idea than Mom reading to me, for a couple of reasons. First, Dad couldn't catch a beach ball if somebody set it in his arms. Second, if I got on a scale holding a dumbbell, it would barely go past seventy. My arms and legs are white, freckly twigs that would probably get stress fractures just from being in the same room as a real linebacker.

"Are you serious?" I say in a disappointed voice, and I can see Dad is a little embarrassed, because he doesn't fight me on it. He pauses and goes, "Um, okay, maybe not football then. You want to hit the Natural History Museum?"

This is a better idea, but it doesn't count, because I'm on to him. He's only doing it because Dr. Greve told him to. "No, thanks. I'm busy."

Like usual, Dad's cheeks give away when he's annoyed. "Oh! You're 'busy.' With what, pray tell?"

"I have homework." He can't argue with that. Before he can come up with another pity plan for poor Billy, who needs more attention so he'll stop messing up the March family's life, I disappear into my room.

Dad's sigh is so loud I can hear it through the door.

I flop on my bed. I wish I could just eat a magic bean and turn into the perfect son so they'd stop bothering me.

Chapter 10

The alarm.

School.

No, it's Sunday.

Church.

I slap the alarm and knock my book off the night table. I try again. This time I hit the alarm, and the buzzing stops. I *hate* the buzzing. I wish it were a fly you could kill just once, and it would never make that horrible sound again. Actually, it is like a fly—an evil zombie fly that comes back to life every morning.

I dig deep under my covers and pull my knees up to my chest. Why does church have to be in the morning? Some people get to go to church in the middle of the week and then do whatever they want all weekend. Some people only have to go for Christmas and Easter. Some people go to temple or synagogue, and I don't think those are on Sunday morning. Some people don't go *anywhere*, they just sleep. . . .

"Billy! We're leaving in fifteen minutes!" Mom yells up the stairs.

The last time I made us late to church, Dad had me go to a movie late the exact same number of minutes.

I shoot out of bed and into the bathroom. Pee, brush teeth, race back to bedroom, pull on suit, pull on shoes—horrible, ugly shoes—race downstairs.

Dad is already opening the garage door.

"Where's my purse? Has anybody seen my purse?" Mom says this at least two times a day.

Finally she finds it, and we're all in the car. I'm jammed between Betty and Adrienne because they're both big liars who say it makes them carsick to ride in the middle. Dad peels out of the garage with a screech. He's obsessed with getting places on time.

Mom turns to look at us. "Billy, did you brush your hair?"

Of course she notices the one thing I didn't do. Not, *Billy, you look so nice in your suit*, or *Billy, I can tell you brushed your teeth this morning.* I touch my hair. It's bad. It's doing the thing. The thing where it gets all staticky and parts are sticking up and I look like a big red fur ball.

"He looks like his hair exploded," says Adrienne.

Mom searches in her purse, but doesn't find her brush. "Adrienne, do you have a brush with you?"

"No."

Mom sighs, and I hear that terrible sound—the *spitting* sound. She's going to slap down my hair with her spit. I don't know why she doesn't realize this is the most disgusting thing ever. "No! Mom, *don't*! That's sick!" I'm ducking, but there's nowhere to go; I'm trapped in girl land between Adrienne and Betty, and Mom's gross spitty hand is swiping my head.

"Billy, hold still. Cut it out."

Dad is actually *laughing.* Mom finally gets me, and I hold still even though I am dying and I want to cut off all my hair and shave myself bald and take a bath in bleach.

"*Gross!*" I yell.

"That looks much better." Mom turns back around.

I can't believe this. I have spit shampoo in my hair. A helmet of loogies. Big, gross green-yellow ones dripping down my ears, pasting my hair to my head.

"I think we made it on time," Dad says, pulling into the church parking lot. Mr. Collins is out by the bell rope, getting ready to ring the bell. If it were me, I would swing on the rope; it's not like Pastor Eric could see.

"Come on." Dad gets out and jets across the parking lot, not really running, but it seems like it, because his legs are so long. Mom's heels go *clack clack clack clack,* and Adrienne whines, "Wait, I can't walk that fast!" and Betty has to run to keep up. Dad pulls open the door just as the bell goes *dong.*

Suddenly everything is slow and quiet and smells like air freshener. We're in the entrance room with dark red carpet and big wooden doors. Dad holds this door open, too, and I walk up the long red aisle to our pew.

I wonder if anybody can tell there's spit in my hair.

I hate going up the aisle. All those people *looking* at me. I know that's what they're doing, because that's all I do: I look at the people who come in, and I think about what weird clothes they're wearing, or I notice their knobby knees or big feet or whatever.

Right now everybody's probably whispering, *Who's that skinny homeless kid with the too-small suit and the weird shoes? Oh, that's just the March boy. They keep him in the basement, except on Sundays.*

I wish I were in the basement right now.

This suit *is* too small. The pants come up to my ankles, but Mom says I'm growing so fast, there's no point in buying me another pair until next year. I hate my ankles. They look like skinny white skeleton bones.

Do they feed that kid, ever? Nah, they just let him catch spiders down in the basement. That's why he's so white; he never sees the light of day.

And my shoes. It makes me sick to know I have them on. They're *shiny*. Not good, polished-leather shiny, like

Dad's shoes, but shiny like girls' shoes, like girls' plastic *purses*. Aunt Diana sent them for Christmas last year, and Mom said we shouldn't waste them, since they're just my size. Mom says nobody in church is thinking about what I look like, but that is a flat-out lie.

I slide into our pew and sit down. I ask God to make Adrienne less annoying, and for me not to be grounded so much. I ask Him to make Todd Anderson stop calling Keenan "Short Stack."

I'm done praying after three minutes, even though I drag it out. I don't understand why church has to be so long.

"Doug, do you have the checkbook?" my mom whispers.

"No," my dad whispers back. "*You* have it."

Mom starts fishing in her purse. It sounds like trash guys emptying a Dumpster, it's so loud. There's all this crackling paper and coins jingling, and Dad is standing there rolling his eyes (he gets embarrassed easily), and finally Mom busts out her checkbook and whispers, "Doug, do you have a pen?"

"No," hisses Dad. "You do!"

They go through this every Sunday. You'd think they'd learn.

Finally Mom finds a pen, and she writes out a check

and tears it off, and of course it sounds like somebody's ripping a whole notebook in half.

"I want to put it in!" Betty jumps for it.

Mom holds it out of her reach. "No, it's Billy's turn," she whispers, and gives it to me.

"Can I do it next time?" Betty asks me.

I nod and she smiles. It's actually kind of a big deal to be the one who gets to put it in when the basket comes around. I don't know why.

I fold the check in half and put it in my pants pocket. It feels important to be carrying around this much money. Good money, to feed starving people and send poor kids to school and stuff. Our church has this village in Mexico where we send money, and the grown-ups go there on trips to build houses and schools.

Not like sending those kids to school is doing them a favor, come to think of it.

"Let us listen to the Gospel," says Pastor Eric.

This is the best part of church. Today the story is about Jesus feeding thousands of people with just a couple loaves of bread and some fish. I wish *I* had something to eat right now. If I could zoom back in time to when Jesus was giving out the fish, I'd ask him for a hamburger instead, and I'd get the best one ever, because God made it, with bacon and cheese, and the ketchup wouldn't be soaked into the bun or anything, and there would be enough pickles for once. . . .

I am so hungry right now. My stomach is starting to do the thing where it feels like it's turning inside out. What if I just . . . ?

No. I'm not going to.

But maybe I could just *look*. So I'll know what we're having later.

See, after church, everybody goes downstairs to the fellowship hall and there's food, usually doughnuts or coffee cake. I could eat five doughnuts right now. Jelly ones, with powdered sugar on the outside and gooey strawberry stuff on the inside. My stomach really is turning inside out. It wouldn't hurt anything if I just *looked*.

I pull on Mom's sleeve. "Can I go to the bathroom?"

"Okay, but come right back," she whispers.

I get out of there.

There's something about being outside of church while church is going on that feels like a party. The bathroom is downstairs next to the fellowship hall, so I go in and make myself pee so God doesn't think I told Mom a lie. When I'm done with the bathroom, I race out to the table.

I don't know why people go to museums when there's

something as beautiful as a box of doughnuts around. The lid is open, and they're laid on tissue like presents: chocolate ones and apple fritters and old-fashioned ones and *jelly* ones, all in little rows, covered with chocolate sprinkles and rainbow sprinkles and powdered sugar.

I lean in and smell.

It's weird, but when you're really hungry, smelling food makes it like you can almost taste it, like it's right there one inch from your tongue, and all you have to do is reach out and—

I touch one. Just a little touch; I barely brush against it, but now there's white on my finger, and I have to lick it off.

I've never tasted anything so good in my life.

Suddenly my fingers are doing something my brain isn't telling them to do—ripping off a little piece of doughnut and popping it into my mouth—and it is the *best* doughnut I ever tasted, fluffy and sweet, and I bet the jelly part is even more delicious. . . .

It would be gross, wouldn't it, to let somebody eat it after I stuck my fingers on it and ripped off a piece?

I mean, what if I have some weird disease like leprosy, and nobody knows yet? I could be the first person to get leprosy since the Bible, and if somebody eats that doughnut, pretty soon their skin is gonna bubble up like bad glue, and their fingers will fall off, and they'll have to ring a bell when they come around so people can run away.

I can't let that happen. I better just eat the whole thing. I lift the doughnut out of the tissue and push a few other doughnuts around to cover the hole.

The first bite might be the best with apples, but it's not with doughnuts. The third or fourth bite is the best, when you get to the jelly and it squirts out and you wish real fruit actually tasted that good.

I take another incredible, jelly-filled bite—

There is a sound. Just a tiny sound, but I whip around, and *the door handle is turning*. I stuff the doughnut in my pocket and grab a plastic cup.

Dad is standing in the doorway. "Billy, you were supposed to go to the bathroom and come right back."

I wave the cup at him. "I was thirsty."

"Well, get a quick drink and come on."

Now I know what they mean in books when they say somebody's heart was racing. I can feel it going *bump bump bump*, doing some kind of weird dance with my stomach. If I hadn't heard him come in . . .

I take a few sips, and we go back to church.

"He was getting a drink," Dad whispers to Mom. That's what being a kid is like: you have two permanent police officers watching you all the time, even when you're going to the bathroom.

Now the choir is singing, and that one old lady isn't here, so they actually sound kind of good.

"Billy, do you have the check?" Mom whispers. The basket is coming around, still a couple rows ahead of us.

I dig in my pocket for the check. My breath whooshes backward. My fingers are plunging into something mushy and wet and goopy, like I reached into my *skin* and hit my own guts. It's jelly doughnut. *The* jelly doughnut. And it's on top of the check, covering it.

The basket is closer now, and my brain is malfunctioning. This is bad. Really, really bad. I push my hand around, trying to get past the doughnut. Maybe the check is dry, *maybe* . . . it's not. It's gloppy and sticky and wet.

I need to decide *now*. Do I put it in, anyway? All that jelly might look like blood, and people will think I'm bleeding to death, and somebody will call an ambulance . . . but probably not. Probably everybody will know exactly what it is, *a jelly doughnut*, and they'll know I was in there stealing doughnuts like some kind of crazy person who takes jam packets from restaurants.

Or I could just pretend I lost the check. I could tell Mom and Dad somebody must have pickpocketed me, there's a thief in this church, better check your purse, and—

"Billy! Get the check!" Mom hisses at me.

I pull out the check and dump it in the basket.

It looks like a soggy, bloody handkerchief on top of all the clean dollar bills and checks. I feel sick. Mr. Morrow, who is holding the basket, stares. Mom and Dad stare. Adrienne and Betty stare. I could run.

Suddenly, Mom's hand darts in and pulls out the check like it's a lit match. A blob of jelly falls to the floor. "I'm sorry," she whispers to Mr. Morrow, and passes the basket to Mrs. Gonzalez. There is a little red, wet spot where the check used to be.

George Washington's face is bleeding.

Mom holds the check between her thumb and pointer finger, and it is a red, gloppy magnet for a hundred eyes—*why did I put it in? Why, why, why?*

"What is that?" she whispers. "*Jelly?*"

"I'll handle this." Dad's hand closes on my arm and he squeezes, a *you're dead meat* squeeze that sends my stomach chasing itself in circles. "Let me see that check."

Mom silently hands him the check, and by now everybody around us knows what's going on; they're all pretending not to look but I can feel their eyes watching me, thinking how weird I am.

Dad is holding my arm so tight I bet I'll have bruises tomorrow. It's not like he has to worry about me running away; there's nowhere for me to go. He pulls me out of church and down the stairs to the fellowship hall.

I'm blinking and trying to walk even though Dad is dragging me twice as fast as I can go, and I don't know how, but our legs get tangled at the bottom of the stairs, and he takes a big lurching step and lands on his bad knee.

"*Dang it!*" he yells, and I know for sure the world is ending, because my dad is screaming in church.

"Sorry." I feel a big choke starting in my throat. I take deep breaths, but it keeps getting bigger.

"Get in the fellowship hall," Dad says.

I go in, and I'm still trying to keep the choke back, and the first thing I see is that box of doughnuts. I wish I could throw every one of them against the wall until the room looks like it's bleeding jelly. I wish I could run away to China.

Dad shuts the door behind us and takes a deep breath. "Sit down, Billy."

I sit on one of the gray folding chairs. *I am not going to cry.*

Dad holds up the check. "What is this?"

Does he not know?

I look at his face for the expression that means he knows the answer already. He doesn't. Of course he doesn't know. Why would he realize that's jelly from a doughnut? Maybe there was a jelly sandwich in my pants when they went to the dry cleaner. It wouldn't be my fault if the dry cleaner didn't check my pockets. I open my mouth to tell him and—

The words shrivel up and die right on my tongue.

I'm in church. God is definitely watching.

But does He care about one little lie? One tiny little lie that doesn't hurt anybody, that just keeps me from getting grounded even longer? I mean, Mom and Dad already grounded me for way longer than they should have, so it kind of evens things out if they don't ground me for this one. If you think about it.

Okay, God?

It's not okay. I don't know how I know; I just *know*.

"It's jelly from a jelly doughnut," I say. "I took one."

Dad looks at the table where the doughnuts are lying and lets out a big sigh. His face kind of droops. "Why, Billy? Why can't we leave you alone for two seconds without you getting into something?"

"I only wanted to look, but I touched one and then I thought, what if I had leprosy so I had to take the whole—"

"Whoa, slow down. *Leprosy?*"

"Yeah, like in the Bible, where the people's fingers and toes rot off and they have to carry a little bell?"

"I know what leprosy is. But why on earth would you think you had leprosy? And what does this have to do with taking a doughnut?"

"I was thinking, when I touched the doughnut, what if I have leprosy and someone else eats the doughnut and gets it, too? So I thought I'd better take the whole thing."

There is a long silence. I tack on in a small voice, "And I was hungry."

Dad is staring at me, and suddenly I feel weird. The air is full of all the secret things he's thinking. He sighs and closes his eyes like he's very tired.

When he opens them, he says in a cold voice that is a million times worse than yelling, "I'm tired of you using your imagination as an excuse. Your problem is you have no self-control. You knew perfectly well what you were doing."

I look at the ground. My eyes are deserts. No rain allowed, *ever.*

I can feel Dad watching me, until my insides are squirming so hard, I just want to shoot off the chair and jet out of there—anything to get away from his stare.

He stands up. "Let's get back in church."

"Aren't you going to ground me?" I whisper. I *want* him to yell and ground me, because that would seem normal. Right now my skin is prickling.

Dad shakes his head. "Grounding hasn't done any good. Your mother and I need to talk about this later. Come on."

There are sirens going off in my head. *What are they going to do to me?*

Chapter 11

"This is called a behavior plan." Dr. Greve pushes the white paper across the desk. "Take a look."

I can't believe they're doing this to me. Like I'm some idiot kindergartner. Even the print is big. I stare at the weird spatter painting on Dr. Greve's wall and think about exactly how long it is until I turn eighteen.

"Just look at it, Billy. Nothing is set in stone." Dr. Greve sounds calm, not annoyed like my mom or dad have been since church yesterday. At least there's that.

I look at the paper. It's mostly blank lines.

I agree that I will_____

_____

_____

_____

_____

_____

_____

_____

_____

_____.

For each _____ in which I am successful, I will earn_____. For each _____ in which I am unsuccessful, I will_____

_____.

Signature _____

Date _____

"You and I can decide what to put on the blanks," says Dr. Greve.

"How about: I agree that I will not be so stupid?" I say, reading from the form. "For each time in which I am successful, I will earn one plate of food. For each time in which I am unsuccessful, I will get a beating."

"Is that what you think you deserve?" Dr. Greve is eyeing me.

"What? No! I was kidding." Is he crazy? What if he really did put that in there? And what if—

Dr. Greve folds his arms across his chest. "I'd like you to think of just one goal, something simple. One way you'd like to act differently."

He's obviously trying to make it seem as if this is all my idea, when really I'd like to make the behavior plan into a paper airplane and fly it into the garbage can. He sure can stare. He has these brown eyes that bore into you like drills. I wonder if they get dry from not blinking enough.

"Okay, my goal is not to mess up anymore," I say, to get him to stop staring at me.

"Let's try to be more specific."

I sigh. *My goal is to move to China and find a new family.* But I don't say it out loud.

"Billy?"

I stare at his desk. I'm starting to hate this place. "Not steal stuff," I say, thinking of the jelly doughnut.

Dr. Greve frowns. "You know, I don't think you're a thief, Billy. That doughnut was an exception."

I look up at him quickly. My parents already told him about that? Of course they did. They probably called him as soon as they caught me.

Dr. Greve goes on. "What happens is that you get carried away in your imagination and you end up hurting things that belong to other people."

"Fine. Not hurt stuff."

"That's good. I think it's just right." Dr. Greve must realize it's not smart to push me anymore, because he starts filling in the blank himself. "I agree that I will not harm property that belongs to others. How's that?"

"Fine," I mumble.

"That means big property *and* little property, okay, Billy? Even a doughnut, or a piece of paper that belongs to somebody else, like a check." He finishes writing and looks up. "Now, I have some good news for you about this next section. Your parents have agreed that for every week that goes by in which you meet your goal, you'll earn a trip to the arcade and ten dollars to play games." He smiles at me. "So let's fill that in, shall we? For each week in which I am successful, I will earn a trip to the arcade."

What? My parents must be really desperate if they're bribing me to be good. I don't want Dr. Greve to see how shocked I am, though.

"Great," I say. "I'll beat *Ninja Warlords* in no time."

He smiles. "That's the idea."

Then something hits me. "What about the next part? What happens if I don't meet my goal?"

Dr. Greve folds his hands. "They're leaving that up to us. What do you think would be fair?"

"Don't let me play video games at home," I suggest.

Dr. Greve raises his eyebrows. "Nice try, Billy. I know you don't have a gaming system."

"Make me the family shoe cleaner, and I have to lick everybody's shoes clean and dry them on my hair."

"Billy."

"Make me wear girls' clothes to school."

"Maybe we should use the suggestion your parents gave me in the event that you couldn't come up with something yourself?"

"I thought you said they're leaving it up to me!"

"Actually, I said they're leaving it up to *us*. They did think you might have trouble choosing an appropriate consequence. But if I share their suggestion, that's the one we have to stick with, so—"

"Take away my TV time," I blurt out, because no way do I want to risk whatever punishment Mom and Dad invented. It's like *Wheel of Fortune*, except there's horrible stuff hiding in the wheel. And TV time isn't too bad a thing to lose since we only get a few hours each week, and Mom and Dad never let us watch the good shows, anyway.

"That sounds reasonable." Dr. Greve talks aloud as he writes. "For each week in which I am unsuccessful, I will lose my television privileges."

"What was Mom and Dad's penalty?"

"I agreed not to mention it, unless we needed to use it."

All of a sudden I'm *mad*. Stupid Dr. Greve and his fake smile and his dumb office are like the old witch's house in Hansel and Gretel, full of stuff kids love but really just a *trap*. Who asked this guy to be my other parent? Here he is, knowing stuff I don't know, having secrets with my parents about me.

"Are you okay, Billy?" Dr. Greve looks worried.

I stare at him, and if I could make my eyes into stun guns, I would.

"Billy?"

"What." My voice is a cold, dead thing.

"I can see you're feeling conflicted about this. That's okay. But don't let your feelings get in the way of your goal. This is a good goal, and I know you can accomplish it." Dr. Greve pushes the paper across the desk. "Why don't you sign it? Then you can give it to your mom when you leave."

I take the pen. *Alexander the Great,* I write. Then, because I already jumped off the cliff, I keep going. *Ivan the Terrible, Vlad the Impaler, Caesar Augustus, Louis XIV, King Hen—*

"That's enough, Billy," Dr. Greve says quietly.

"I'm not signing it because it's not my goal!" I yell. "You made me do it, so it doesn't count!" It's the rudest I've ever been to Dr. Greve, and I kind of hold my breath, waiting for him to blow up.

But he doesn't.

He leans back in his chair and looks at me. "You're right."

The earth shivers. A couple of stars implode. Did he seriously just admit I was right?

"I'm sorry if I pushed you too hard." He sounds so calm. "I was excited because I thought it might be a good way to help you work on some of the things causing you trouble. But if you're not ready to try this, that's okay, too."

My madness starts to evaporate. Dr. Greve is just trying to do his job. It's not his fault my parents can't manage their kid and I can't manage my life.

"This contract is only good if it means something to you. And if it doesn't, then it's nothing but a piece of paper." Dr. Greve moves to throw it away, and suddenly it's like I can see a good, well-behaved me going right into the garbage can.

"Hold on," I say.

His hand stops midair.

But I can't think of anything to say to him. I don't actually think I *can* be good, even if I try my hardest.

Dr. Greve frowns, like he just realized something. "You know what else we shouldn't have decided without you? Your reward. Your parents assumed you'd like the arcade, but I think we should have talked to you first. Is there something special that you've always wanted? Or an activity that you'd like to do more often?"

I stare at him. There are so many things I want, I can't possibly list them all.

But what do I want *most*? Easy.

"A phone," I say.

He frowns. "I don't know how your parents would feel about that."

"My sister got one when she was ten. I wouldn't even need data in the plan," I say quickly. "I just want one that can shoot video." I *would* be good if they'd give me one of those. I'd handcuff myself, if I had to.

Dr. Greve looks up. "Video? Why is that?"

I shrug. "I don't know. I like to make movies and stuff."

"Hmm." Dr. Greve writes something on his pad. "That might be a good creative outlet."

"Yeah, I need an outlet." Little does he know I'm pulling the biggest heist in history right now. There's no way Mom and Dad would get me a phone unless a doctor told them to.

"So when did you get interested in making movies?" Dr. Greve asks.

"My dad got a new phone last year, and he let me film stuff with it. Then I accidentally erased some important stuff, and he said I couldn't use it anymore."

Dr. Greve's eyebrows go up. "Interesting. Let me talk to your mom for a minute, okay?" He leaves me alone in the room, and I squinch my eyes shut and pray as hard as I can. *Let her say yes, let her say yes, let her say yes.* . . .

He's back after a few minutes, with a smile on his face. "Your mom is on board, Billy. But she was very clear that data won't be in the plan."

"That's okay!" I say. I seriously might pop, I'm so excited. I can't believe my mom went along with this.

"So let's change this part, shall we? For each week in which I am successful, I will earn the right to keep using my phone." He looks up at me when he finishes writing. "What if you think of yourself as a film director? Directors have to assess the set, the actors, everything in the room. They're not operating alone. So when your imagination starts making a movie, I want you to consider how the movie will affect other people and the set. Remember our goal? No hurting other people's property?"

I nod.

"Well, if what you're doing in your movie might cause that to happen, it's a *cut*."

"Okay," I say quickly. Before he can change his mind, I grab the behavior contract and sign below the king names: *William Blake March, aka Billy the Kid.*

Dr. Greve smiles. "I have to say, Billy, it's nice to see a kid so excited about a behavior contract. I think the phone was a good idea."

It sure was. Bribery is a *great* idea.

Also, not that I'd ever admit it, but part of me would like to be a kid my parents can be proud of. I'm positive it's impossible, but if there's even a flea-speck chance that signing this thing might help my stupid brain control itself, I'll try.

Mom doesn't say much about the behavior contract when I come out of the office and give it to her. She just glances at it. "This looks like a good plan, Billy. You have a talent for making movies." She gives me a sly look.

"You saw my chocolate milk movie?"

She nods. "It was pretty funny, mister. But now that you're getting your own phone, don't play with mine again."

"When can we get it?" I ask.

She smiles. "How about right now?"

It's like I entered some alternate reality where I have cool parents. I nod fast, and she starts laughing.

"This is your early birthday present," Mom tells me as we're leaving the store. I'm carrying my phone in a little plastic bag.

"But I wanted a skateboard!"

"Well, you'll just have to settle for a phone." Her lips have that squinched look that Adrienne calls "cat butt." I better not say anything else.

My birthday. I'll be eleven in a couple weeks. I can't believe I'm getting so old, and at the same time, I can't believe it's so long until I'm eighteen.

"Billy." Mom glances at me as we pull up to a stop sign. "Do *not* go waltzing into the house with that thing, showing it off. I want you to let *me* tell your father about this."

"Okay," I agree. Mom can be very strategic. Half the stuff I know about managing people, I've learned by watching her.

"And understand this: if you get in any trouble, I'm taking the phone away."

This worries me. "Like *any* trouble?"

"Any trouble that hurts a person or property," says Mom.

I try to think about what trouble I *am* allowed to get in, and I can't come up with much. I have a feeling I won't get to keep this phone for very long. I brush the thought out of my head. I *will* keep it. I'll be good, and I won't mess up, and my parents won't take it away.

I play with my phone the rest of the way home. The camera is completely awesome. It's very simple:

just *record*, *fast forward*, and *rewind*, and a system for trashing and zooming. With this thing, I'll never be bored again. I can make awesome documentaries right in my room.

Maybe I'll do an exposé on messed-up families that are nicer to their daughters than their sons.

Mom pulls into the driveway. "Remember what I said?"

I shove the phone into my pants pocket and pretend to zip my lips.

Mom starts laughing. "You don't need to go that far. Just don't wave it around."

As if. I'm not doing anything that'll get this thing taken away.

I zoom into the house and head upstairs. I'm going to start my exposé. I shut the door to my room and start getting ready. It's important to look pathetic, so people feel sorry for me. I'm already halfway there from my genes; it's hard to believe somebody as skinny as me actually gets fed enough. To make myself look even skinnier, I put on a giant T-shirt that Uncle Frank gave me, a 49ers shirt.

Look how sad. The kid's wearing a football jersey, and he's about as big as a real football player's femur. And he doesn't even own a pair of pants.

Then I take the blanket and sheets off my bed—a bare mattress is always sad—and wad up another T-shirt at the top, like it's the only thing I get for a pillow. Now I need some dirt for my face. If I had any guts, I'd scrape some off the bottom of my shoe, but that's too gross, even for me. Wait: I have a newspaper article on my bulletin board, about Dad winning a big case. I take it down and rub it all over my cheeks, especially under my eyes.

I'm ready to shoot. I prop up my phone on the dresser and turn on the camera, then jump on my bed and scoot back, all hunched up like I'm cold.

Just then the door springs open and I almost fall off the bed. "Billy?" Dad sticks his head in. "It's time for din— What are you doing?"

"Nothing!" I squeak, hoping he doesn't notice the phone.

Dad shakes his head. "I don't even want to know. Put your sheet back on your bed and come down for dinner. And wash your face! What *is* that?"

"Just dirt," I say.

Dad looks like he's going to say something else, but then he sighs and pulls the door closed. I switch off the phone.

Guess I won't be using *that* footage.

Chapter 12

Family dinner is the worst idea anybody ever came up with, if you ask me. Families are bad enough already, what with lumping together all these people who didn't get to pick each other—except Mom and Dad, I guess. They got to pick each other a long time ago. But they didn't get to pick their kids, and kids don't get to pick their parents *or* their brothers and sisters. So for a kid, family dinner is this time when you have to sit around with a bunch of people you probably wouldn't even talk to at school.

I wish I at least got to pick a brother. I'd pick one skinnier than me, with even brighter red hair, so I'd look normal next to him. He'd be really cool and smart, but he'd be younger than me, so I'd always be just a little bit cooler and smarter. We'd play practical jokes on Adrienne and Betty together, and we'd have bunk beds and this system where we talk through Morse code by tapping on the bunk. His name would be Huck. (Ever since I read *Tom Sawyer*, I've wanted a friend named Huck.)

"Billy, come sit down." Dad is cutting the pizza. He makes pizza once a week, and it's pretty bad, but none of us want to tell him. Lately he's been making whole wheat crusts, which are even grosser and doughier than regular ones.

I pull out my chair and sit.

"How did it go?" Dad asks Mom in a low voice, as if we all don't know that by "it" he means my appointment with the head doctor.

"Great," says Mom. "We came up with a good plan. We can chat about it later."

Betty says, "Billy's crazy. Adrienne told me."

I can feel my face heating up—boiling—and it's all I can do not to reach across the table and punch her bratty little face in.

"Girls! I don't *ever* want to hear that word used about your brother again. Both of you apologize," says Mom.

"Sorry, Billy," says Betty, and Adrienne mutters, "Sorry," but she's not even looking at me.

I sink my teeth into a piece of pizza, letting sauce smear all over my face. What if I were a lion and Adrienne were a zebra, and she had to be afraid of me all the time? I rip into the pizza harder and chew with my mouth open, staring right at her. *Next could be you*, I think.

"*Gross!*" says Adrienne. "Mom, look how Billy's eating his pizza. He's so disgusting."

Mom glances at me. "Billy, wipe your face. That is disgusting."

I wipe my face and take a big swig of milk to wash down the fresh kill.

Betty squinches her nose. "I hate pizza. It's gross."

"Betty, don't talk that way about your food. This is wonderful pizza." Mom is such a liar. I can't believe she's always telling me not to lie, and then she tells a crazy whopper like this. But I'm so hungry I take another piece, even though it does taste like canned Spaghetti-O's on raw dough.

"I'm just trying to cook for my family," Dad says in a hurt voice.

"I know, honey, and it's delicious. We love it." Mom looks at us kids like, *say something*, but nobody does. So Mom keeps digging herself deeper, lying away. "You got the sauce perfect tonight. Did you put something new in it?"

"No." Dad takes a sip of water. "You know, never mind this cooking thing. We'll just get Papa John's next week."

"Really?" says Adrienne, and Betty goes, "Papa John's!"

There is a long silence.

Ha. For once I'm not the idiot who said the wrong thing.

"I like your pizza better, Dad," says Adrienne, but it's way too late.

"I don't," says Betty. "I like Papa John's."

Dad silently takes another bite of pizza, and so do I. Us men. Surrounded by girls all the time. Girls who don't know when to be quiet. Girls who are bossy.

I know everybody says I'm gonna start liking girls *that way* soon, but I don't believe it. If I do, I'll just get married to Mary Kazowski, because she doesn't talk a lot. We'll have a silent family, who lives together but doesn't say dumb stuff all the time like this family.

What if I really couldn't talk? What if aliens did an experiment on me and took out my eardrums and voice box?

"Mom, Billy's putting his napkin in his ear!" says Adrienne. "He's so *weird*!"

"*You're* weird, you mangy zebra," I tell her.

Dad starts laughing. He must have had a good day

at work, because normally he wouldn't think that was funny.

"Why are you putting a napkin in your ear?" Mom reaches over to pull out my earplugs.

There's really no good answer for that.

"Because he's crazy." Betty looks at Adrienne. "Remember, you said he was crazy?"

I feel sick. I make my eyes into slits and glare at Adrienne. Sometimes I really hate her. Betty is probably the only person in the world other than Keenan who sometimes thinks I'm cool, and now Adrienne is ruining it.

"Stop it, Betty!" says Mom. "Use that word one more time, and you'll go to your room."

"But Adrienne said it first!"

Dad sighs. "Let's play the quiet game, okay?"

The quiet game is a stroke of genius Dad came up with a couple years ago when Betty learned how to talk and we all realized she was going to be one of those people who never shut up. Basically, whoever can stay quiet the longest wins, and if you make a sound you lose a point. That's the "game."

For a while we eat in silence, and then the others start talking again. But I stay quiet. I can't believe Adrienne has been telling Betty I'm crazy.

Finally Dad says, "Come on, if everybody's done. Let's leave the dishes for later and have some family time. I think we need it."

Oh no. Family time.

It used to be fun, when I was, like, five and still thought Adrienne was cool and Betty was cute. But now it's torture. Mom and Dad are obsessed with us spending time together, and they keep trying to *make* it work, even though obviously nobody's having fun (except maybe them, in some weird parent way).

"But I have homework," Adrienne says.

Dad shakes his head. "You never have homework when you want to go out with your friends. Family time is first priority." When he gets like that, there's no point arguing.

I go to the living room and grab my favorite corner of the couch before anybody else can get it. Mom sits in her recliner, and a couple seconds later, Adrienne stomps in and throws herself on the other side of the couch so hard that if it were a seesaw, I'd go flying up in the air. Then Dad comes in holding something behind his back, and Betty follows him with a bunch of spoons.

"I thought we needed a treat." Dad sets a carton of pecan praline ice cream on the coffee table. "Betty, make sure everybody gets a spoon."

"Dad! I can't eat that, it's not organic," says Adrienne. She recently started caring if things are organic or not. Mom says it's one of the problems with living in Seattle.

"Then we'll eat yours for you, and you can have some whipped tofu or something," says Dad.

I grab a spoon and dive in, because the pralines are the best part and I want to get as many as I can before Dad starts hogging them.

"I guess I'll have a *bite*." Adrienne pushes her spoon in. Her "bite" is more like a whole scoop.

Dad and Mom and Betty stick their spoons in, and for exactly one second family time is perfect, because we each have ice cream, and nobody is saying anything at all.

Then Betty licks her spoon and says, "Tell stories about us!" That's something we always do at family time; Mom and Dad tell us funny stuff we did when we were little.

Mom smiles. "I remember one time when you were two, Betty, I left you for a second to get the phone, and when I came back you were on top of my dresser, eating diaper ointment out of the bottle."

"Gross!" Betty squeals in delight, as if we haven't heard that one a million times. "Another one!"

Dad says, "How about the time Billy cut up our sheets, making Betty into a mummy? I think he'd been reading too many Halloween books."

"Or when Billy filled Adrienne's shoes with glue and cheese because he was trying to catch mice. Remember that?" says Mom.

"Those were my favorite shoes," Adrienne says in a snotty voice. "Every story about Billy, he's ruining something."

It's not that big a comment. I know it. But for some reason it makes me so mad that my eyes feel bloodred, and I wish I could make my hands into laser guns and blast her. "You're a big fat.jerk and Ben will never like you!" I scream, and race upstairs.

"Billy!" calls Dad. Weirdly, he doesn't sound mad. More worried.

I go into my room and slam my door. I hate them. I never should have been born into this family. God messed up. My real family is in China, wishing for a kid like me. I look at my phone, sitting on the dresser. Forget the movie I started earlier; I have a better idea.

I take my suit jacket out of my closet. I hate it even worse than my shiny shoes, but Mom and Dad make me wear it to weddings and fancy parties. I put it on and set up my phone. I take a few steps back and make my voice friendly, like a guy in a commercial.

Her name is Adrienne March, and she's thirteen years old. She is the perfect kid. She never messes up or gets in trouble. For example, she would *never* make your shoes into mousetraps. But she *would* polish them, and do the dishes, and whatever other cleaning stuff you need done. She lives at 980 48th Avenue in West Seattle, and she likes caramel popcorn, so you might want to try using that to get her into your car.

I hit *stop* because I'm starting to creep myself out. What if some kidnapper accidentally saw this and *did* kidnap Adrienne—it's not like I actually want that to happen. I know real kidnappers do a lot worse stuff than make kids clean their houses. I go ahead and erase it because you never know.

Making the ad did make me feel better, though.

I take off my suit, pick up *White Fang*, and crawl under my covers. But I can't concentrate on the book. My head is whizzing with ideas for movies, commercials, interviews, and documentaries.

I'm still thinking about movies when Dad comes in to say good night. He sits on the end of my bed and pats my foot. "Sorry about your sisters, buddy. They weren't on their best behavior tonight."

"It's okay," I say.

"Your mom told me about your new phone. Think you're going to be able to stick to your end of the deal?" My dad loves deals.

"Yeah," I say, sitting up in bed. "And I'm going to make cool movies with it. I decided I'm going to be a movie director when I grow up." Actually, I just decided that this second. I look at him to see what he thinks.

He has a weird look on his face. "That sounds like fun, kiddo. I'm sure it'll be a nice hobby. But it's not a smart job to aim for."

"Why not?"

"No job security. Too many guys out there all trying to do the same thing." He scrunches my foot. "With your big old brain, you could do anything you want to. Something in the sciences, or even law like me." He looks hopeful.

I don't say anything. I want to make movies.

Dad sighs and gets up. "Anyway, buddy, let's stick to your end of the deal, make sure you get to keep that phone, okay?"

"Okay," I mumble, and lie back down.

Chapter 13

When I wake up the next morning, the first thing I
see is my phone. I have a billion ideas popping out
of nowhere, like my brain was working while I was
asleep.

I could do a documentary on what really goes on in
the school bathrooms during recess. I could get some
footage of Tommy McCrory talking pervy about Miss
Andreevna, and film Cesar Gutierrez making first
graders say, "I pledge allegiance to Cesar Gutierrez . . ."
Or me and Keenan could go around and ask kids,

"What's the weirdest thing you ever saw a teacher do?" We'd show teachers, mug-shot style, and then cut to a kid answering that question. Except we'd be completely dead if we did either of these ideas.

What would be safe, but still funny? Maybe a documentary showing how messed up kids' lives are, with everybody always telling us what to do. I could call it *A Day in the Life of a Kid.*

I'm so excited about starting, I get out of bed even though there are still a few minutes before the alarm goes off. Mom laid out jeans and a T-shirt on my chair, but instead, I dig through my dresser for the Bad Sweater. Everybody has one. Mine has a reindeer on it, with a pom-pom nose and candy-cane antlers. It's kind of creepy.

I put it on along with my plaid long johns, the ones Aunt Leah gave me last year on Christmas Eve, because Mom and Dad like to make us dress up on Christmas morning and pose for pictures like we just *happened* to be wearing brand-new matching pajamas to bed.

I set up the phone on the dresser and turn on the camera.

Being a kid is like being in jail for eighteen years. You don't get to pick what you wear.

The door opens, and Mom pokes her head in. "Billy, your bre— What are you wearing? You're going to be too hot in that."

I pull off the sweater. It's so bad, I'm embarrassed for Mom to see me in it, even though it was *her* sister who gave it to me. "Yeah, I know. I was just trying it on."

Mom frowns. "Um, okay. Breakfast is ready." She disappears down the stairs.

I get dressed in my normal clothes and bolt downstairs to do my next take. Mom left a plate of toast and eggs at my place, but it looks way too nice. Lucky for me, Adrienne's almost done eating.

I peer over her shoulder. "Can I have those?"

"My *crusts*?"

"Yeah, I need them for something."

Adrienne looks at me like I'm a complete weirdo, but she stands. "Yeah, I'm done. You have to clear my plate, though."

I move her plate to the floor, arrange the crusts a little better, and scrounge around for some dust bunnies. There are always a few under the china cabinet. I set a good hairy one on top of the crusts, and then hock up a loogie and spit it in my empty cup, like maybe that's the only thing they're giving me to drink.

Then I take out the phone and position it on a chair.

"You are a *freak*," Adrienne says, like she's just realizing it for the first time. "Has anybody ever told you that?"

I'm so happy about my phone that I just smile and turn it toward her. "Say that again, okay?"

She yells, "Mom! Billy is being weird and taking pictures of his breakfast!"

You can hear Mom sigh from the kitchen. A minute later she comes into the dining room. I've already put the crust plate back on the table.

"He was filming those." Adrienne jabs her chin at the crusts.

Mom looks like she's about to say something to me, but then she pauses and turns to Adrienne. "Billy's allowed to use his phone however he likes, as long as he's not hurting anyone. I want you to mind your own business."

POW! KAZAM! Old Adrienne looks like she just got punched in the kisser. I soak it up, because moments like this don't happen too often.

"Both of you, hurry up. We're leaving in five minutes." Mom points to the clock.

I stuff a few bites of eggs into my mouth and run to the kitchen to get the thing I need for my final scene: some tinfoil. A good long sheet of it. I fold it carefully, stick it in my backpack, and zip my phone into the front carry pouch.

This last part is going to be good.

I get to school ten minutes before the bell. On nice days, kids are supposed to stay on the playground until the bell rings. On rainy days we jam into the cafeteria. Today is drizzling, which doesn't count as rain in Seattle, so I scan the blacktop for Keenan.

He's messing around, doing sprints. I race over to him and scream, "They call him the Road Runner!"

He winds down and comes over to me, panting. "That's lame, man."

"The Tornado?"

"Nah, the Bullet."

"Okay, the Bullet. Dude, you're never going to believe this."

He grins and wipes the sweat off his forehead. "What?"

"Check it out." I drop my backpack onto the pavement, unzip the front pocket, and pull out my phone.

Keenan's eyes get big. "Where'd you get that?"

I smile proudly. "My parents got it for me. They're bribing me to be good."

He laughs. "In your dreams."

"I'm serious. It was the shrink's idea."

Keenan knows when I'm for real. His jaw drops open. "I gotta get my dad to take me to this guy. What's his name again?"

"Dr. Greve. You should tell him you want to try a behavior contract. That's where they pay you to be good. You can pick anything you want; it doesn't have to be a phone."

"But I'd have to start getting in more trouble for him to want to do that," Keenan says thoughtfully.

"Yeah, that's true," I agree.

Keenan's not naturally bad like me. He's a pretty simple guy. He likes numbers and running and chess, and if you let him mess around with those things for the rest of his life, he'd be perfectly happy and never cause any trouble at all. But he's definitely not "good" either, or I probably couldn't be friends with him.

Then I see a little gleam of tinfoil peeking out of my backpack, and I remember what I wanted to do before the bell rang. "You want to check out the phone?" I ask.

Keenan's got it in his hands practically before I'm done asking. Dude loves technology. He could take apart a computer and put it back together in the time it takes most people to brush their teeth.

"Careful," I tell him. "Don't let a teacher see."

Keenan nods and keeps fiddling with the buttons.

I get busy with my tinfoil. First I roll it into a long snake. Then I rip it a little so there's a weak spot in the middle. I bend the ends to make circles and stick a hand through each circle. Tinfoil handcuffs.

"Put it on camera and record me for a second," I say.

Keenan checks out my handcuffs and starts laughing. "What are you doing?"

"It's the last scene of this movie I'm making. Just hit the button in the corner. Yeah, that one. And keep it pointed at me, okay? Make sure you get the school in the background."

I don't need to tell Keenan twice. He starts filming.

Keenan lowers the phone, cracking up. "What is this for?"

"I'll let you see it later," I promise him.

Just then, the bell rings. I shove the phone into my pocket, because I'm not dumb enough to wave it around inside the building, where anything except paper and pencils is fair game. I bet the teachers sell all the stuff they take from us on eBay.

We stop in our class for attendance, and then me and Keenan and a couple other kids go to the resource room for G.A.T.E. It's only once a week for an hour, but it's so boring, it feels like a whole day.

"After school, let's make a movie with your phone," Keenan says as we head into the resource room.

"Yeah!" is all I have time to say, because Shelley swoops down in a cloud of her too-sweet perfume with a big smile and says, "Hello, boys!" Today she's wearing a long purple skirt and about a hundred silver bracelets on her arms.

I'm not trying to be rude, calling Shelley by her first name. She told us to do that. Personally, I don't like it when grown-ups want kids to call them by their first names. It's either wannabe or fake, and actually now that I think about it, Shelley is kind of both. She's always telling us how "special" and "talented" we are, right before she gives us photocopies of some brainteaser and goes off to mess with her Kindle in the corner.

On good days, we get toothpicks and marshmallows or modeling clay instead of brainteasers. Today we're supposed to build a bridge that can support as much weight as possible. We did this last year. There are only eight of us in this class, and the other six are girls. No offense to them, but Keenan and I are way better at building stuff.

I knock out my bridge in like ten minutes and then I start a spaceship.

Raquel leans in for a look. She's always bugging me. She's one of those "perfect" girls, with her hair in a tight ponytail, and her papers all organized, and bright white sneakers. I don't trust anybody whose sneakers stay white longer than a few days.

"What's *that*?" she asks. If she can't see it's a spaceship, I don't know what she's doing in this class.

I cover it with my arm. "None of your business."

"It looks like a dreidel," she says, kind of snotty.

I give her an annoyed look and check out *her* bridge. "Well, that looks . . ." I trail off. She's broken all her toothpicks into pieces and paved her bridge in geometric patterns. She even mashed up marshmallows and made sculptures at each end of her bridge. ". . . like it couldn't hold a flea," I finish, hoping it's true.

"It can," she says smugly. "It can hold fifty-three Hershey's bars." She looks at my bridge. "I don't think yours could hold that much. See where the marshmallow is coming off at the side? That's where it's going to break."

I scowl at her and turn back to my project. What this spaceship needs is a cannon. I hollow out a couple marshmallows and connect them with a tube of side-by-side toothpicks. I may be bad at bridges, but I'm good at guns. I give it an experimental puff—yep, works fine—and lay a toothpick inside. Blowgun.

Wait—I have a better idea. I break up a toothpick and stick on a marshmallow full of tiny spikes, then attach it to another toothpick. *Mace* blow gun. I guess these were medieval aliens.

I look over at Raquel. She's working on another marshmallow sculpture now. Little does she know that extraterrestrial terrorists have invaded her country and are about to attack.

I picture an alien raising his tentacle. "Fellow Plutians, the reign of the evil Earthling queen is about to end! Long live King Mog, Terror of the Intergalactic Seas! And . . . fire!"

I lift the cannon to my lips and—

I think about my phone, sitting in my backpack. Mom just paid a hundred bucks for that thing, and it was supposed to cure me. If it were recording me right now, it wouldn't show aliens. It would show me blowing a toothpick-mace into Raquel's neck.

It was a dumb idea, anyway. Real aliens would never land in a school.

I set down my gun.

I always get caught doing bad stuff, but nobody ever catches me being good. I guarantee Dad would be happy if he knew I didn't shoot a toothpick-mace at Raquel. But it's not like I'm going to tell him. I wish he just magically knew.

And then I get an idea, one of those ideas that's so cool it's practically sending off sparks. I poke Keenan.

He looks up from his bridge, which is even better than Raquel's. "What?"

Just then, Shelley puts down her Kindle and says, "Who's ready to share their bridges?" Of course Raquel's arm flies into the air.

I guess I'll have to wait until after school to tell Keenan. That's okay. It just gives me more time to plan.

"I don't know, man," Keenan says after he hears my idea. "It sounds kind of dumb." We're walking down

Admiral, getting ready to turn onto our street. Our school is only four blocks from where I live, and six blocks from Keenan's house.

"You're only saying that because you're not in it!"

Keenan shrugs. "Yeah, maybe."

"Well, what if we do one about you next? We could do a documentary on the making of an Olympic track star."

I can see Keenan likes that idea, because his eyes get that half-asleep look they always have when he's planning something.

"You could wear those new Speed Sharks for the scenes where you're running," I tell him. Keenan is *obsessed* with having the latest, best running shoes.

"Huh," he says.

"And we could show you drinking muscle shakes and doing sprints on the sidewalk."

Keenan says, "Why not on the track at the playfield?" and I know I've got him.

"Because that looks too good. We have to show you, like, overcoming challenges. It would be even better if we could go into one of those bad neighborhoods and have you running on a sidewalk full of broken beer bottles and stuff."

"Yeah," Keenan breathes. "That would be dope."

"But let's do mine first," I say, because we're getting to my house, and I need him to decide.

He shrugs. "That's cool."

We head inside. It's very quiet. I check the message board, and *yes,* Mom left a note saying she's at book club. I have no idea why grown-ups would do home-work when they don't have to, but she's into it.

Keenan looks a little disappointed. He likes Mom. She's always trying to push food on him and talk to him about his teachers and stuff. I think she feels bad for him. Keenan could probably get a lot more mileage out of the no-mom thing, but I've never brought it up. It's kind of a delicate subject.

"Come on!" I tell Keenan, and we race upstairs.

I dump my backpack on the bed and grab the phone. Keenan goes, "Let me see that for a second," and before I know it, he's recording my pillow and talking in this creepy voice about the ghost of Old Man Jones.

I whack him. "Cut it out. You're supposed to film me."

He turns the phone toward me. "Action!"

"Not yet, foam brain, I have to get supplies." I actu-ally spent the last hour of school thinking about this, and I know exactly what I need for the first scene: Drano and bleach. Mom keeps that stuff in the laundry closet, which is down the hall, so I get both bottles and bring them back to my bedroom.

Keenan gives me a weird look. "What are you going to do with those?"

"It's something for my parents. Just record me, okay? One, two—"

He holds up the phone.

Keenan starts cracking up, so I swipe my hand across my throat and he stops recording. "Oh, man, are you seriously going to show this to your parents?"

"Yeah. It'll prove a point. Hold on while I get the matches."

"Oh, *man!*" says Keenan. I can hear him cackling from all the way down the hall while I go to my parents' bathroom and get the matches on the candle Mom uses for her baths.

"This one's going to be even better," I say when get back to my room. I tear off a match and get ready.

"Action!" Keenan starts recording again.

I *could* set my closet on fire so I could play firefighter, but I *don't.*

I know I'm not supposed to play with matches. So I *don't.*

By now, Keenan is giggling so hard that I'm pretty sure he's ruined it. "So when can we start my movie?" he asks when he finally calms down.

"Maybe tomorrow. We can take the bus to one of those sketchy neighborhoods after school and film you doing sprints."

Keenan frowns. "I don't know if it's such a good idea to wear my best kicks in a hood like that."

Hmm. He has a point. "Well, then we need some beer bottles and cigarettes that we can put on *our* sidewalk. We can get them out of somebody's trash."

"Cool!" Keenan gets that half-asleep look again. "I'm going to do some laps right now. If I don't train every day, I'm never going to make it to the Olympics."

"Keenan, chill. It's just a movie."

He raises his eyebrows like, *Oh yeah?* And he takes off. "Later, man!" he hollers from halfway down the stairs.

I flop on my bed. I have to laugh. Maybe he really will win the Olympics some day. You never know with Keenan.

Chapter 14

After Keenan leaves, I mess around in my room for a while; do my homework, read some more *White Fang*. Finally I put the book down because I'm starting to get hungry, like, gnaw-your-own-finger-off hungry. Too bad there's only gross food in the fridge.

What I really want is cookies, but they're locked up. My parents are so weird. I guess I could microwave a burrito. I climb out of bed and head for the kitchen.

I'm halfway down the stairs when I hear voices.

I freeze—and then I realize it's just Adrienne.

And a guy. That's a guy's voice! Who is it?

I go the rest of the way down the stairs and peek around the corner.

What the heck? Adrienne's on the couch practically sitting on a guy's *lap!* I mean, not exactly *on* his lap, but she's right next to him! Their legs are definitely touching. I can only see the back of their heads, but he looks big. And he has dreads! I never saw a white guy with dreadlocks before. In fact, I never saw anybody with dreads except Bob Marley, and that was just in a picture. These are the real thing—big furry logs of hair hanging around his shoulders like gigantic yellow worms. How does he *get* them like that? Glue, maybe.

Or maybe gum. I bet that's what Ben does—that has to be Ben—he gets a huge pack of bubblegum, the kind that comes in a pouch like chewing tobacco, and he chews it into big wads and rolls his hair around it until he has gigantic bubblegum-hair-worms. They would be pretty sticky, though. I wish I knew for sure.

I bet I could find out.

They're both facing the window. If I walk really, really quietly and stay against the wall, I could touch the back of a dread. They're so busy talking they won't even notice. Hair doesn't have nerves, right?

I inch forward, putting my heel down first and then my toes really slowly, so I'm panther-quiet. . . . In fact, I might *be* a panther. I'm a lean, hungry predator out for meat. My vision is razor sharp, zoned in on the bubblegum-worms dangling in front of my nose. My claws slip out—and I touch one.

Ben practically explodes off the couch. "Hey!" he yells. Suddenly he and Adrienne are staring at me.

"Brat!" shrieks Adrienne.

"Whoa," says Ben. "I didn't hear him coming."

"I didn't know he was home," says Adrienne.

"Sorry." I back up quickly.

Ben looks weirded out. "What were you doing?"

Adrienne glares at me. "You're such a freak. Get out of here *now*."

I start to say no, and then I see Ben looking at me. He's pretty big, to tell you the truth. And he's wearing weird clothes, what Mom would call *Seattle clothes*— raggedy jeans and this too-big shirt with leather fringe on it.

Like an outlaw.

One of Billy the Kid's enemies.

I shoot upstairs pretty fast, but I don't actually make it to my room. I kind of lurk on the landing, right out of sight. Who is he, anyway? I still remember the names from last year: Buckshot Roberts? Jimmy Dougherty? He's probably going to rob Adrienne and then kill her, like those guys used to do.

I ease around the top of the landing and poke my

head out. Billy the Kid is on the prowl. Target sighted: the evil outlaw Buckshot Roberts, sitting next to a teenage girl, about to do another horrible murder. What I need is my magic bullet. I jet into my bedroom and dig a baseball out from under the bed.

But . . . should I?

The baseball wants to leave my hand so bad it's practically talking to me: "*Pleeeease* throw me, please!"

Then I think of my phone. But this isn't *damaging* anything, only surprising Adrienne a little bit. She deserves it, for calling me a brat. It's not like I'd throw it right at them. I'd aim for the wall, and I wouldn't throw it too hard. Just enough to bounce off and scare them.

Still, I can see my name just how I wrote it on the contract: *William Blake March, aka Billy the Kid.* Something about signing a contract makes things more serious. I lower my arm. I can't believe I'm missing this good chance. But I seriously don't want to lose the phone. It would be just like my parents to write an extra clause into the contract, in invisible ink or something: *No throwing balls in house.*

Then old Ben leans in and *kisses* my sister—a sick, goopy, slobbery dog kiss with his tongue!

I rear back and hurl that sucker, 350 mph, straight for the wall above their heads.

The ball catches the corner of the mirror and—*crash*—it falls!

"Aaaaagh!" Adrienne screams.

I am running as fast as I can into my room. *Oh crap. Crud, crud, crud. I hope she's not hurt.* I'm so stupid I can't even hit a wall when I'm trying.

What if she *is* hurt? I definitely heard glass breaking. I can't hide in here if Adrienne is bleeding to death. What if I have to call an ambulance?

I take a deep breath and run back out of my room and downstairs and peek around the corner.

"You little jerk!" Adrienne yells. She and Ben are standing up, picking glass off themselves. There's a heap of glass on the couch. Adrienne has blood on her face, and Ben is bleeding from his arm.

"Should I call nine-one-one?" My voice comes out in a croak.

"You should call the morgue, so they can pick up your body when I get through with you," says Ben, and he doesn't sound like he's kidding.

I jet back upstairs. A few minutes later, I hear the door slam.

Maybe they're going to the hospital.

I go down to the living room and try to clean up the glass. But it's hard because my hands are shaking, and there are so many tiny pieces in the couch and carpet. It's like the mirror exploded instead of just breaking. I do my best with a plastic bag, and then I put pillows around the area so nobody will step on it.

I go back to my room. I should walk around the yard and soak up my last minutes of freedom, because once my parents hear about this, I'll be locked up until I'm twenty-one. But I'm so freaked out, all I want to do is lie on my bed. I try to slow down my breathing and keep myself from crying.

I really screwed up this time.

Waiting for Mom and Dad to get home is the worst torture ever—worse than getting tarred and feathered or put in the stocks. The house is dead quiet. I can't get the horrible picture of Adrienne's face out of my mind. She was *bleeding*. Probably the number one thing, the biggest thing Dad has ever taught me, is *never hurt a woman*. He's said that at least a million times.

And I definitely hurt Adrienne. He's going to kill me.

I don't have that long to wait. Adrienne must have called them, because when Mom has book club, usually nobody gets home until six—but it's way before six when I hear the door *slam* open and hit the doorstop downstairs. No matter how mad Mom gets, she never opens the door like that.

Then I hear voices: first Mom, and then Adrienne answering her.

She's okay, I think as I hear my sister's voice. I'm so relieved that I take a shaky breath—*thank You, God*—and I realize I was actually more worried about Adrienne than I was about getting in trouble.

Maybe Dad's not home after all.

Thud thud thud thud thud thud.

He *is* home.

He's coming up the stairs, and my head is seriously going to explode, I'm so scared. I jump off the bed and hide in the closet, but it's too late. I'm just closing it when my bedroom door flies open and my dad yanks open the closet and growls, "Out."

His face is the shade of red that only red-haired people get—so bright it hides his freckles—and his blue eyes are popping. "Billy!" he yells. "We just got back from Urgent Care! Adrienne might have a permanent scar on her forehead! Her friend is getting stitches in his arm right now! I am *sick* of your behavior!"

A permanent scar?

"He wasn't even supposed to be here!" I yelp. I want to tell Dad about him kissing Adrienne . . . but I already put her in the hospital. I don't need to get her in huge trouble, too.

Dad's chest is heaving. He slams his hand against the wall, and I can tell he wishes it were my face. "No, he wasn't, but that's none of your business! You had no right to attack him and your sister!"

I am frozen. I would run if I could, but he'd catch me.

He clenches his hands into fists. "You are not allowed to ruin things for this family, do you understand? If you want to screw up your own life, go right ahead, but you will *not* hurt your sister and her friends, do you understand me?" His voice is so loud my eardrums might shatter.

"Doug."

Dad jumps.

Mom comes into the room. "Easy, Doug. Let Billy tell his side of the story."

Dad glares at her like *she* was the one who did something wrong. "He doesn't have a side! There's no excuse for hurting his sister! And you know what? That rip-off artist isn't getting any more of our money. Billy's getting *worse.*"

I feel sick. Rip-off artist? He must mean Dr. Greve.

"We just got started. It takes a while, Doug." Mom's voice is supersoft, like she's trying to calm a raging pit bull.

"No, I never liked this idea from the beginning. I'm not paying someone to *talk* to Billy when what he needs is a spanking! If he can't behave like part of this family, he can leave!"

I wish I could disappear. I wish I could burn up right here. I always knew he wanted me gone. Now he's admitting it.

"Doug!" Mom's eyes have a dangerous look.

"Stop defending him! We spend all our energy dealing with him, and the girls get shortchanged!"

My breath feels funny, like I can't pull in enough air. Everything keeps coming back to this totally obvious thing that I don't want to believe, but that I know is true: my dad hates me.

"Doug!" Mom snaps. "You need to calm down before you deal with Billy. Take a minute!"

"Don't tell me what—" Dad cuts himself off and stalks out of the room.

Instead of yelling at me, Mom comes over and tries to give me a hug.

I push her away. I feel like I could throw up. He admitted it. He doesn't want me in this family. He said I could leave.

"Billy, your dad didn't mean what he said. You know he's just upset about what happened. Give him time to cool down."

"Go away," I say, but I can barely get it out. I'm crying, and I *hate* crying, but I can't stop.

"Billy," Mom says in a gentle voice.

"Go away!" I scream, and she finally does, and shuts the door behind her.

I sit on my bed. I'm shaking.

I hate him so much I could explode. I look at the phone on my dresser. I can't believe I wasted time making that video with Keenan. I'm glad I wasn't stupid enough to show it to him. He would think it's the dumbest thing he's ever seen.

I'm going to run away.

The thought sinks in, getting bigger and stronger in my head.

I am going to run away.

Uncle Frank and Aunt Diana want a kid, but something is wrong with Aunt Diana and they can't have one. Dad said they're thinking of adopting. Well, they can adopt me. They're rich because they're both doctors, and they're never home, so I wouldn't annoy them too much. I'm going there tonight.

Dad said I should leave. So I will.

I'll take the bus. Adrienne takes the 56 downtown all the time with her friends—but I don't know how to get to Uncle Frank's. He lives in Madison Park, and that's at least two bus rides away, maybe three.

I try to make myself breathe slower. I have to make a plan. Everything will be okay; I'll look up the bus route online. They'll see me if I go downstairs, so that leaves Adrienne's computer. Her room is right next door. Before I can chicken out, I open the door and run for it.

Adrienne's computer is a beat-up old Dell that used to be Mom's. I type in our wireless password and Google "Seattle bus directions." The first link is Metro Transit trip planner. I don't know Uncle Frank's address, but I do know he lives near the corner of Madison and Mc-Gilvra. I type that in. Then there's a little box where I have to put in what time I want to leave. When will they be in bed?

I enter *10:00 p.m.* The screen shows a timer and then directions. There's a 56 picking up at 10:15 on Admiral, four blocks away. If I take it downtown and switch to an 11, that'll get me a few blocks from Uncle Frank's. I can walk the rest of the way. A shiver runs down my back. I'm really going to do this.

Click.

Too late, I jump away from Adrienne's desk.

"What are you doing?" She's standing in the doorway, glaring with one eye. There's a bandage over the other one.

Dad's right. I'm a piece of junk.

Adrienne opens her mouth, and her voice comes out like an ambulance siren. "Mom! Dad! Billy's in my room messing with my computer!"

Really fast, I click the X in the top corner to close the computer screen. I've learned my lesson about leaving up screens.

"Mommmm!"

I run out of there and dive onto my bed.

A minute later, Mom opens my door. "Billy, what were you doing in Adrienne's room?"

"Looking up something for homework." The lie jumps out of my mouth.

She sighs. "We have a family computer for that. Right now is not the time to pull stunts. Your dad is already upset."

I turn over and face the wall.

"Don't leave your room again, unless it's to go to the bathroom. Your dad needs time to cool off." She pauses. "I'll bring up some food in a little while."

I glare at the wall. Pretty soon they won't have to keep me locked away. I won't mess up their nice little life anymore. I hear a click as Mom shuts the door.

Now I need to pack. I should have done this a long time ago.

Chapter 15

Ten o'clock takes a million years to get here. First I have
to eat dinner while I'm listening to *them* eating without
me. I can't hear much, just forks clinking. Then Dad
laughs really loudly at something Adrienne says, and she
starts laughing, too.

They're having a great time without me around to
mess it up.

There's water running while they do the dishes, and
finally Dad comes up to get Betty ready for bed. I can
hear him talking to her in the bathroom about her "pet"
elf. They're trying to think of a name for a creature that
doesn't even exist.

"Kookoo-naka." Betty's always saying stuff like that, just weird sounds, not real names.

Dad plays into to it. "How about Baba-googoo?"

Betty giggles. "No, Fafa-leelee."

And on and on they go. It makes me sick to hear how much fun Dad is having, how happy he sounds, like he doesn't care that his other kid is locked up next door.

I think about the real Billy the Kid, and how his stepdad didn't want him either. When his mom died, his stepdad dumped him in a foster home. That's when Billy started getting in trouble.

Finally Dad's and Betty's voices disappear into her room. I get out of bed and take my phone off the dresser. I was just going to leave and let Uncle Frank call them when I got to his house, but now I have an idea. A video I want them to see. I need a few things, and it will only take a minute. . . .

A little while later, I hear Mom say good night to Adrienne. Then she peeks in my room. I'm lying under my covers with the lights off. My backpack is ready in the closet. "Good night, Billy," she says.

My heart gives one quick jump, and I have a sad, horrible feeling of already missing her, but I cram it back down. I keep my eyes shut.

Mom pulls the door closed again.

Then things get really quiet. I hear the *tick tick tick* of my clock sitting on the nightstand. I wonder if they'll miss me. I want to think that they will, but then I remember what Dad said about me taking attention away from Adrienne and Betty, and I know they won't. They'll be relieved I'm gone.

What will they do with my room? Maybe Mom can have the craft room she's always talking about. But what about my stuff? I guess Uncle Frank can pick it up—or maybe he'll just buy me all new stuff. He's rich, and I'd rather have brand-new stuff, anyway.

Then I think about my sisters. Adrienne will be happy. But Betty . . . she's the only one in this family who doesn't hate me. Good old Betty. I wish I could tell her good-bye.

I need to do this before I wimp out. It's nine forty-five, but I can't wait any longer. I get out of bed, quiet as a ninja, and slip on my backpack. Then I open my door slowly, slowly, pulling the handle so it doesn't click . . . and slide into the hall.

I am a ghost.

A sneak thief.

A stealth glider.

There's a crack of light under Mom and Dad's door, but other than that, the house is dark. I creep downstairs, stepping on the outside of each step and skipping the noisy ones.

I can't believe I'm really doing this.

I glide into the kitchen and dig in my pocket for my phone. I made a movie for Mom and Dad. I don't want them thinking I got kidnapped and calling the police or something. I set it on the counter and scribble on the message board: *Press play on my phone.*

Uncle Frank can pick it up later.

Then I go through the living room to the back door. I look at the handle, but I sort of don't want to open it. I take one last look around our living room—at our comfy couch, and the bookcase full of our favorite books and movies, and the fireplace mantel that's filled with all kinds of junk we've made over the years. There's Adrienne's teapot that looks like a broken watering can, and Betty's pipe-cleaner picture frame, and the mouse house I built with Dad in third grade. It's so crooked no mouse would ever want to live there. I don't know why they kept it.

For some reason all this stuff is making me sad.

I could turn around right now and go back to bed, and nobody would know. I don't *have* to do this. Am I chickening out?

I think of Dad's words. *He can leave. We spend all our energy dealing with him.* I put my hand on the door handle and turn it. Maybe I'm a little loud, I don't know. I stop and look at the stairs. Will they come get me?

I sort of kick the door. Just lightly.

Nothing. They don't care.

I step outside and pull the door shut and start walking fast, with my head down and my hands stuffed in my pockets. It's raining lightly, only a sprinkle. I'm not scared, even though it's black out here. Our neighborhood is so safe you could probably leave a bag of a hundred dollar bills in the street and somebody would go door-to-door, trying to figure out who it belongs to.

It doesn't take me long to reach the end of 48th, which puts me onto Admiral. That's the main street that leads to the West Seattle Bridge, and then downtown. It's practically a highway, with so many cars whizzing through, even late at night.

I go to the closest bus stop and lurk behind some bushes, keeping an eye out for the 56. I don't want to think about what would happen if one of our neighbors drove by and saw me standing here. In West Seattle, everybody knows everybody.

Headlights stream past, lighting up the hill. I'm feeling kind of weird right now, a little bit chicken. My stomach is doing the twisty thing.

I try to calm down by thinking about Uncle Frank's house, and how great it's going to be. I'll have the downstairs guest room, which has its own rainforest shower, and a big-screen TV with a whole bookshelf of movies, and the best-smelling soap I ever used. Aunt Diana is like that. And they'll buy me a skateboard, so me and Keenan—

Keenan.

I don't want to live far away from him! If I move in with Uncle Frank, Keenan and I probably won't go to the same school anymore. But maybe I can take the school bus and still go to school in West Seattle. Yeah, that's what I'll do.

There's a humming, grinding sound, and the 56 climbs over the hill. *Whreeeeee.* It pulls over to my stop. The doors open with a puff, and a couple of people get off.

This is it.

I take a breath, climb the steps, and dump my money in the slot, keeping my head down so the bus driver can't see my face and say, *Hey, what are you doing out by yourself on a school night? And why do you have a backpack the size of a car?*

But he barely seems to notice me. I hurry to the back of the bus, the second-to-last row. I scoot against the window and pull my hood over my head and squinch up, like if I make myself small enough, nobody will see me and wonder what I'm doing.

The bus starts again with a squeal, and we pull into traffic. I'm still freaked out, but there's a bubble of excitement in my chest. I pulled it off. I actually did it.

Later, suckers. I won't be messing up your lives anymore.

We grind up Admiral to California, which is where Metropolitan Market and all the restaurants and stores are. Grown-ups are streaming past, coming out of restaurants and standing outside Admiral Theater. I'm starting to realize there's another world that happens after kids are in bed, when all the grown-ups go out and play. The ones that aren't stuck at home watching us kids, anyway.

Now we're through the intersection and on the long glide down Admiral onto the West Seattle Bridge. There's something about crossing the water that makes it final. No more familiar West Seattle; now I'm going downtown, where things are dark and there are homeless people all over the place, drinking from paper bags and asking for money. Especially in Pioneer Square.

I'm a little nervous about switching buses there.

I stare out the window at the lights slipping by and the construction guys working at night. We're over the bridge and on First Avenue going downtown.

I hope Uncle Frank and Aunt Diana will be happy to see me. Uncle Frank always said I was his favorite nephew, although I'm his only nephew, so I don't know if it counts. They'll probably call Mom and Dad when I get there, but I'm sure I can convince them it's best for everybody if I move in. They want a kid so bad, and Mom and Dad don't want me.

It's perfect, if you think about it.

We pass the giant Starbucks building and the fire station. The buildings are getting closer together now, with streetlamps on every corner. We're almost at Pioneer Square, and I see lots of people through the windows. Some of them are wearing blankets or giant dirty backpacks, and some are just sitting on the ground.

I get a weird choky feeling as the bus pulls up to the big triangle on First and Yesler with park benches and the trees wearing weird knitted sweaters. This is where I'm supposed to switch buses.

Why did I do this again?

I think about Dad yelling at me. I think about Uncle Frank's house, and my own room, and the big-screen TV . . . but it's not working. I want to jump out of my skin as I walk down the bus steps into the cold night air.

It's loud out here and full of grown-ups who look like they're up to no good. I stand right next to the bus sign: number 11, coming in ten minutes.

Number 11. Ten minutes. All I have to do is wait.

It's so loud out here. Somebody shouts a cussword, and somebody cusses back. People are laughing in a scary crazy way. All the sounds are blending together: voices and glass clinking and cars roaring and footsteps.

I keep my head down and hook my thumbs through my backpack so nobody can rip it off my back. I could punch myself in the face for doing this. I am so dumb.

"You got some change, brother?"

I keep staring at the ground, hoping he's not talking to me.

"Hey, you got some change? Our car broke down, and we're just trying to get a bus ticket. Hey, kid! You hear me?"

I look up. It's a guy with a ponytail, wearing ripped jeans and a dirty white T-shirt even though it's freezing out here. He's skinnier than a person ever should be, with wide-open dark eyes. There's something wrong with him. He's shaky, moving around fast, switching from foot to foot. Next to him is a long-haired old guy in army clothes. He has a paper bag in one hand. I know what's in that bag.

"Hey! I'm talking to you!" says the skinny one. "Come on, we need some help! You got some change? What you doing out here, anyway? You're just a kid. What you got in there?" His eyes flit to my backpack and then to my face. "You got a couple bucks?"

I can't breathe. I take a step back and he says, "He won't answer me!"

The guy in army clothes says, "Leave him alone, Jay. He's scared."

The skinny guy spits on the ground and walks into the park. He looks like a dirty, bony ghost. After a minute the other guy follows him, and I'm alone at the bus stop again. My legs don't feel right. I sit on the bench and stare down the road, and everything is blurry. I pray harder than I've ever prayed for anything for number 11 to pull up.

"Hi."

I almost jump out my jacket.

A guy sits down next to me. He's old, like my dad's

age, with long gray hair and stubble, and he's wearing a ripped dirty suit. There's plenty of room, so why did he sit so close to me? I scoot to the edge of the bench.

"Where you headed?" He smiles at me.

"To see my uncle," I whisper. *Please stop talking to me. Please go away.*

I can feel his eyes digging into me like arrows. "Yeah? Where does he live?"

This isn't right, him asking me questions. Somehow I know he wants more than money. My breath is coming fast, and I feel numb.

A bus pulls up, but it's number 18, not 11. I want to scream for help to the bus driver, but my voice won't work. The doors puff open, the driver gives us a bored look, and then the doors hiss shut and he pulls into traffic.

"What's your name?" the man says, moving closer. He sets his hand on the bench right next to me, almost touching my leg.

I can't answer. I can't even think. My heart is going so fast it feels like it might burst out of my ribs. I have to run. But he's so big. What if he chases me? I stand up, and—

Whoop! Whoop! Blue and red lights flash. There's a police car coming down First Avenue. For one crazy second I think, *God sent it to protect me, and the cops are going to chase this bad guy away*—but of course they couldn't know.

Then the police car pulls up to the bus stop and the front door flies open, and . . . *my dad gets out!*

"Billy!"

The weird man next to me gets up and walks away fast.

I jump up, and Dad swoops me into his arms—and he's crying, really crying. He goes, "Billy," and hugs me so hard. I see a cop get out of the car behind him. I'm shaking, and I can't seem to stop.

"Billy," Dad says again. "Thank God." He's shaking, too, and his face is pressed against mine. I hug him back. All this relief comes bouncing out of my body like a big clown with a hammer and—*bonk*—bonks me on the head. *You big dodo, he* does *love you.*

Finally Dad sets me down, but he still keeps an arm around me, holding me to his side. The policeman is speaking into his walkie-talkie.

"We have to call your mom." Dad pulls out his cell. A second later he says, "We found him. He was at the change point in Pioneer Square." I can hear Mom start to cry on the other end of the phone. "We'll be there in fifteen minutes." Dad hangs up.

The cop puts his walkie-talkie back in his belt. He frowns at me. He's tall and kind of young, with spiky brown hair and glasses. "That was a stupid thing to do, Billy. A boy in Everett ran away last month, and you know what happened to him?"

Dad holds up his hand. He's got his courtroom look. "Thank you, Officer, but I think he's scared enough. I'll handle this."

The cop shrugs. He nods at the car. "I'll take you home."

"Thank you." Dad holds open the door for me, and we sit in the backseat together. I wouldn't normally admit this, but he holds my hand the whole way home.

When the cop pulls up to our house, he says, "You'll need to sign a statement." He clicks on the ceiling light and writes for a few minutes on a clipboard, then hands it back to Dad.

Dad writes for a while, while I rest against him. It feels good to be next to him, leaning on his big shoulder, smelling his *Dad* smell. I don't know why I ever thought I wanted to go to Uncle Frank's.

Finally Dad gives the cop the clipboard and hands him a card. "Call me at the office if there are any loose ends."

The cop glances at the card, and his eyes get just a

tiny bit wider, the look anybody in law enforcement gets when they realize Dad works for one of the best firms in King County. "Yes, sir. Metro Transit Authority is filing a report, too, so they may get in touch, but I think I've got all I need. Have a good night." He glances at me. "Stay out of trouble, Billy."

I nod.

My dad thanks the officer again, and the car pulls away from the curb. Then Dad puts his arm around my shoulders and leads me toward the house. Before we even get to the sidewalk, the door flies open, and Mom comes hurtling out, with Adrienne right behind her.

I get smooshed all over again. Mom is hysterical.

Even Adrienne hugs me. When she does that, I almost feel like crying. She should hate me for messing up her face. It's a big bandage. I can't believe I did that.

"I'm sorry about your face," I tell her, and she hugs me tighter.

"It's okay. I know it was an accident."

Finally Dad says, "Easy, let him breathe. Let's go in and sit down."

Mom keeps her arm around my shoulders as we walk inside. "Where's Betty?" I ask, because for some reason I feel like I was gone a month, not an hour, and I want to see everybody, I'm so glad to be home.

"She's asleep." Dad shuts the door behind us. "Adrienne, why don't you head up to bed? Your mom and I need some time with Billy."

Adrienne nods. She squeezes me on the shoulder and says, "I'm so glad you're okay." Then she's gone, and it's just me and Mom and Dad.

"Let's sit down," says Mom. "I'll make hot chocolate."

Dad says, "Billy, you're wet. I'll get your pajamas." He and Mom look at each other, and Mom goes, "The chocolate can wait," like she's scared if they leave me alone for one second, I'll disappear again.

Mom and I sit down while Dad goes upstairs. She doesn't say anything, just holds me close and rests her cheek against my head. "You scared us, buddy," she says quietly.

"I'm sorry," I say.

She hugs me tighter. "Don't ever do that again, okay?"

Then Dad comes down, which is a relief, because Mom is sliding into Mushville fast.

But Dad has a weird look on his face. He's got my pajamas in one hand, and with the other, he's holding out my crumpled suit and Adrienne's yellow plastic wig from when she dressed up as a Ken doll for Halloween. "Billy, I found these on your closet floor. Were you trying these on for something?"

I stare at him. Doesn't he know? "They're from the video I left you, remember?"

Dad frowns. "What are you talking about?"

"The one on my phone that told you I was going to Uncle Frank's. I wrote on the message board for you to watch it."

"We didn't get that message," Dad says slowly.

I'm confused. "Then how did you know where I was?"

"We searched the history on your sister's computer," says Mom. "We remembered you were in there, so we checked and found the route map."

"Oh." My voice is an atom. So they didn't see the video. Maybe that's a good thing.

Dad disappears into the kitchen and comes back with the phone. "You left us a message on *this*?"

I give a little nod, and Dad turns it on. Maybe I should stop him . . . but there's a tiny part of me that wants him to see this. He stares at the screen. Mom gets up to stand next to him. Then I hear my recorded voice start to speak, and Dad practically drops the phone.

Dad and Mom look at each other like two cartoon characters who just got whacked with a two-by-four. *Dongggg*. You can almost see the birds flying around their heads. The room is very quiet.

Finally Dad says in a weird voice, "Billy, why did you choose the name Stanley?"

"Because Mom said that's what you wanted to name me."

The world is going to implode any second now, because my dad is crying for the *second* time tonight. He pulls me off the couch and practically crushes me in a hug. "Billy, I don't want Stanley. You're my son, and I don't want any other. Do you understand?"

Then Mom puts her arms around me *and* Dad. I wriggle, but not that hard. "We love you so much," she says into my hair.

"Uh, yeah," I say, because I'd say anything to get them to stop. There's been way too much crying tonight, and it's freaking me out.

Dad finally lets me go. "I know I get mad sometimes, but I wouldn't change anything about you. And I *love* the name Billy. It's way better than Stanley, okay?"

"Okay," I mumble.

"And I can't think of anything worse than having you gone." Boy, Dad is really grinding it in.

"What about when I'm eighteen?" I say. "Or thirty? *Then* will you want me gone?"

"Maybe when you're thirty," says Mom.

Then I think of something. "How did you know I left?"

Dad looks sad. "It didn't feel right to go to bed without saying good night to you. I wanted to tell you it was okay; I knew it was an accident and you didn't mean to hurt Adrienne."

For some reason, when he says that, all these feelings bust loose in my chest. "Yeah," I say. "It *was* an accident. Lots of stuff I do are accidents. I feel like you never see when I'm good, only when I'm bad. And I don't know if I even *can* be good. I'm trying, but . . ."

I stop talking. It's hard to explain, and it makes me tired to try.

But I can see from Dad's face that he understands. "I know you're trying, buddy. You don't have to be perfect. We all make mistakes. The important thing is that you keep trying. Can you do that?"

I nod. I *can* do that. I can be very stubborn, when I want to.

For a minute, me and Dad look at each other. I know one thing for sure: I'm never running away again.

Then Dad gets this look that I totally understand—
there's too much emotion going on for me—and he clears
his throat and says, "How about we have that chocolate
now?"

"I'll get it ready." Mom heads for the kitchen.

I sit on the couch, and Dad sits next to me. He picks
up the phone and turns it over. "You know, Dr. Greve
has some pretty good ideas."

"Yeah," I say.

He glances at me. "Do you think he'd mind if I
came along next time you go see him?"

I stare at him in shock. "Are you serious?"

Dad nods. "Maybe we could go together. I think he
could help us keep talking."

"I thought you said he was a rip-off artist."

Dad turns red. "I was wrong about that."

"Oh," I say. "Okay, then." And I'm not even bummed
that I have to keep seeing Dr. Greve. If Dad is coming
with me, it won't be so bad. Besides, I don't really mind
the guy. He got me a phone.

Dad sets it back on the table. "If you like this filming
thing, we'll get you a real video camera, if you want."
I look at him to see if he's serious, and he's staring
thoughtfully at the phone. "Remember when we used

to do those pretend interviews with my phone? You loved that."

"Yeah, that was when I was in fourth grade," I say. "Then I erased your files and you wouldn't let me use it anymore."

He looks surprised. "Good memory. Well, I was thinking, maybe we could do something like that again."

"But not pretend," I say. "I'm old enough to do real movies now."

Dad laughs. "Yeah, okay. We'll do a real one."

"I'll think of a good part for you," I promise him, and he laughs again. But then he says, "Stick with this filming thing, kiddo. You've got a good imagination."

You know what? I think I will stick with it. My dad knows practically everything, and if he says I should, then I know it's true.

Chapter 16

"So there was this *pervert* that tried to kidnap me, but the cops came and arrested him, right at the very second he was going to drag me away."

Keenan leans against my bed and gives me a suspicious look. "You're lying, man."

"Well, I *did* run away. And there *was* a pervert."

"For real?"

"Yeah. I was running away to my Uncle Frank's house because my parents were being jerks, and this creepy dude tried to talk to me in Pioneer Square, but then my dad came and got me."

Keenan stares at me. "How'd he find you?"

I shrug. "I guess they searched the history in Adrienne's computer, so they could tell I was looking up the Metro schedule, and my dad came in a cop car to where I was supposed to change buses."

Keenan looks amazed. "A cop car!"

"Yeah. The cop was trying to scare me, talking about some kid who ran away and got killed or something, but my dad made him be quiet."

Keenan snorts. "Dude, you're a fool. What are you even running away from?" He waves his hand around.

I look around my plain, old, boring room. "What are you talking about?"

"You got sweet digs, you got all this cool stuff, you got cool parents . . ." He trails off.

We're both quiet, and I know we're thinking the same thing: he doesn't.

Then Keenan goes, "So your parents didn't take away your phone or anything?"

I shake my head.

"Does that mean we can do my track video?"

I look at the phone sitting on my windowsill. "Yeah!"

Keenan gets a gleam in his eyes. "Cool."

"I think we should do an interview with you right after you won the Olympics, wearing the medal and all, and then cut back to shots of when you were a kid," I tell him. And then, oh man, I have the best idea! It's flowing into my brain like electricity, and I'm so excited I laugh out loud.

"What?" says Keenan.

"I'm going to do one of me, too!"

Keenan gives me a weird look. "No offense, but you can't run that fast."

"Not running, stupid." And I explain.

Keenan loves it, like I knew he would. But before we can start shooting, we have to get supplies, and stuff for the set and costumes, too.

We collect:

The recycling box from under the sink.

A liter of Coke.

An old T-shirt that we rip up so it's mostly scraps of cloth hanging off a collar.

Sunglasses.

The fur coat that Grandma gave to Mom but Mom never wears because she says it's made out of poor baby minks.

Adrienne's soccer trophy.

A piece of blue ribbon.

Yellow construction paper.

Ketchup.

Thirty-two peanut butter cookies, which we promise Mom we won't eat.

Keenan's best running clothes and kicks.

A bunch of beer cans and cigarette butts that we sneak out of Mr. Weatherby's trash and recycling.

A cardboard box.

A stick.

A red bandanna.

It takes us about an hour to set everything up outside on the lawn, but we're finally ready to film. Mom has been checking on me every five seconds since I asked her for the cookies and the fur coat. Finally, when she sticks her head out the back door *again*, I say, "Mom, if you don't trust me, I'll never learn how to be good."

She thinks about that for a second and says, "All right, but you're cleaning up everything when you're done." Then she goes away.

Me and Keenan look at each other, like, *yeah* and we get rolling. Real fast, we crunch up Mr. Weatherby's beer cans and throw them around on the sidewalk. I scatter a few of his nasty butts, too.

We're here today with Keenan "the Bullet" Biggs, five-time winner of the Olympic gold in track and field. Keenan, how does it feel?

Really good, man.

Let's take a look at how Keenan got to be the Bullet. Here are some clips of him back when he was a kid, dreaming of Olympic gold. Keenan practiced all the time, and he never gave up, no matter what.

So you practiced a lot, Keenan. Anything else?

I took care of my body, and I ate a lot to keep up my energy. I kept hydrated, too.

Shouldn't it be milk or something? Don't real athletes drink milk?

Real athletes drink Red Bull and Coke. It makes you go faster.

I can see his throat working like mad—he's gonna do it!

The Bullet just chugged a whole liter of Coke! And that's Keenan Biggs, five-time winner of the Olympic gold!

Now we've got an interview with Billy the Kid, the famous act—

Film director!

Oh yeah, film director. Billy, how'd you get so good at making movies?

I practiced a bunch when I was a kid. But my first real movie was *Runaway*. That one got an Academy Award.

Something bad happened to the kid who ran away, but you have to watch the movie to find out what.

You're the youngest director to ever win an Academy Award. Anything you want to say?

Yeah. Thanks, Mom and Dad, for putting up with me. Thanks, Adrienne and Betty, for being my sisters. Thanks, Dr. Greve, for getting me started being a film director.

See you in the movies!